CYBORG REDUX

21st Testing Protocol Book 1

IMOGENE NIX

ISBN 978-0-6481205-1-3

For my Family

Prologue

Clarissa's eyes closed, her body arching against the radiated agony. Every muscle quaked while the sound of harsh breathing—*hers*, her grasping brain shared—teamed with a rapid, beeping crescendo. One last, fraught beat of her overtaxed heart saw the mechanical echo segue into the single, unceasing whine of a heart monitor flatlining.

Her last thought was *I'm dying*.

Chapter 1

The beep of the heart monitor attached to the woman on the gurney became the whine of flatline as techs rushed the room. The surgeons working frantically pushed them away.

They hadn't come to save her, but to harvest body parts and defined organs—the bits that would be discarded when she underwent the bio-organic therapies outlined by Dr. Jeremy Colvert. She wasn't the first by any stretch, but certainly the most promising specimen he'd come across. Of course, the therapy process had to be covert. Not everyone understood or welcomed his take on a brave new world.

Beyond the room, on a suspended viewing platform above, Jeremy watched, satisfied with what he saw as the medical technicians began the multiple surgeries. The slicing of the flesh, exposing what to him were unnecessary organs, satisfied him immensely. They hurried, hands flying, blood spurting, while inserting chips and wiring. Organs for transfer were stowed into cooler boxes for transportation, yet others discarded.

The assistants replaced her liver, damaged in the accident that had stolen her previous life, with a technological replacement of smooth metal and prosthetic bio-organic materials, which were crafted just for her.

Each move was a dance, carefully orchestrated, and Jeremy braced himself against the glass. "This one should be successful."

The surgical intern beside him—his personal assistant—glanced at him and shrugged. "Who knows. So far, we've had only limited success."

Ah yes, limited success. How I detest that term! This time will be different though. He clenched his fist, aware of the curling and the interest in that action from the man beside him, but it only lightly impinged on his senses. Everything else, every fiber of his being, remained focused on the procedure taking place in the room below.

Three had died. One had resurrected, but the brain deficiencies were too extreme, resulting in the need for termination of the speci-men. A shame really, as he'd been strong in his body. For a moment Jeremy recalled the soldier they'd chosen. So very strong, and yet the mind had utterly failed, and even to this point, the transplant of brain and consciousness was tricky. Things would be better this time, as he'd chosen this girl himself.

Those working below—the best and brightest of those committed to his cause—

continued his work, taking care with the completion of their tasks. The cooler blocks they'd placed around her body ensured no degradation of the specimen as they prepared her for resurrection, just like a phoenix in his mind. Even as he watched, the cooler boxes of discarded organs were whisked away.

He grunted, looked back to the operating table, and considered once again the only other survivor. "We should check her pain threshold when she is revived. See to it." His work with others had born out his belief that those who'd undergone this new and exploratory therapy could tolerate pain more than those un-enhanced. "Make it work."

Jeremy turned and glanced at his hand, silver glinting under the dim lights of the viewing platform. The *whir-clank* of his personal hydraulics system filled the air.

If only I'd been a candidate. His own injuries had left him with two cybernetic legs, a cyber-enhanced hand, and a hunger to build bigger and better. It had ended his official surgical career, but not his brain capacity, though he'd managed to mask the extent of his injuries from those he groomed.

Those same injuries had pushed his work underground where he practiced and perfected with only the most damaged candidates. The ones society and the medical community deemed to be beyond assistance. In the early days he'd worked on grafting of bio-technical fusion, which had led to other, far more lucrative, endeavors. Now he was ready to move to the next stage, some nineteen years after his first successes came about.

Self-funding, thanks to his judicious work and investment, allowed him a new level of freedom. The medical community at large turned a blind eye to his experimentation, especially since few realized the extreme limits he was prepared to go to in search of his view of purity.

Others—and he included those in government—lacked imagination. *They limit themselves*, he thought and chortled before leaving the room and heading for his office where he'd work on his latest batch of refinements.

THE GIRL in the surgical bed opened her eyes and blinked, lids opening and closing in

quick succession while her vision flashed blue and white. *I died. Why am I here? Who am I?*

It was a struggle, her mind logy with drugs she somehow understood were being pumped through her body even before she noted the steady stream of something being injected into her

arm. "Who am I?" she said, the words strange and harsh.

Clarissa. It came to her as did the reality that her body was different. It felt heavy and

alien, yet stronger. *Strange.*

The small thought exhausted her, and she slipped back into unconsciousness, waking again some time later. "Where... Where am I?" She licked her dry lips, felt the cracked sting as the parched flesh was moistened.

The beeps echoed. They were sounds she recognized, and Clarissa glanced up. The ceiling above her was bright white and dotted with harsh fluorescent lighting.

She stretched, aching down to her bones as unfamiliar sensations flashed through her. "What..." Her throat closed, and it took a moment to force the moisture from her mouth down her throat. "What happened to me?"

A voice echoed in her mind. "Clarissa, you're awake. Wonderful. I'll send a technician in to check your fittings."

Confusion filled her. *Fittings? Technician?*

She waited, her body not vibrating but the shaking close to it. Sensations overwhelmed her, although she did detect a renewing of her strength, while information flooded her mind.

Information scrolled across her vision, yet there was no screen before her that she could detect. Panic set in, her breathing speeding up.

"Be calm," that disembodied voice instructed.

A hiss sounded and cool relief released muscles that had tensed. Anxiety floated away. A door opened, but she couldn't move her head; it remained constrained in a contraption

that held every limb and body part still. The terror that flooded her system felt far away as she struggled for the correct word to describe the contraption that held her in place. *Vise.* It felt like the vise her father kept in his small workshop at the back of the house.

"Where am I?" she asked.

A technician with a white smock and cap popped into her vision joined swiftly by another. "You're in the Colvert Clinic. Remember?" Their smiles seemed odd, like they were watching for some kind of negative response and reaction. She sensed a tension about them, as if they were suffering from an adrenalin surge.

"What happened to me?"

"I'm not at liberty to discuss that with you. You'll need to meet with Dr. Colvert at a later

time. He'll explain everything."

The technician scurried around, tapping details into a hand-held computer, tugging on

cords though not releasing her. Clarissa struggled, fear ballooning again in her chest, pushing against her lungs, and she heaved, trying to suck in oxygen. Terror surged.

"Breathe slowly. It'll help." That voice came again from elsewhere, stern and strong.

Stars exploded in her vision, and she struggled, fingers curving but not grasping anything. "I can't..."

Confusion warred, her heart rate speeding if the monitor's klaxon and the sudden heaviness in her chest were anything to go by. She felt as if she would burst. Perspiration dotted her upper lip.

"Breathe, dammit! Control your oxygen intake or you'll sleep again." The faceless tech's voice echoed, and she fought against the sensation that Jeremy was somehow there, inhabiting her brain. The wild thought scattered to the four winds as Clarissa tried to regain control of her body and mind.

"I want out of here!" Her weak cry was married with a burst of terrifying emotions. Hot tears dribbled down her face as she heard the man cursing.

Once more cold trickled in her veins and the gray fog loomed. "No! I don't want to sleeeee..."

Chapter 2

Michael twisted, his hand moving smoothly, clasping the tennis racquet. He'd always taken this for granted; now every action had to be considered, planned down to the most minute details. He forced his body to react as it has always done instinctually.

He was growing used to his infirmity, and the level of detail required to instruct his muscles to move wasn't so exaggerated, yet now he knew the calculations continued in his brain without conscious thought.

"Very good, Michael. You're coming along well, though I notice your battery levels are very low. Have you been plugging in as regularly as you should?"

He considered the woman's words with distaste. She treated him as if he were some kind of walking, talking toaster!

"Michael..."

He sighed with resignation. They'd had this argument many times since his accident. "I don't realize they're so low until the critical light glows."

It was ironic his friend Sara—a cybernetic implantation specialist—had saved his life after the accident damaged most of his organs and bones. She'd saved him, but the offside was extensive cybe-organic transplant. *Cutting edge.* But now he wasn't who he'd been before, and he continued to wrestle with the emotional price tag that carried.

"How long until I can leave the facility?" he asked.

Sara stared at him. "You're still in initial treatment, Mike. You're vulnerable to infection and—"

"I'm not asking for a medical list of reasons why not, I just want some kind of ball park as to when." Frustration exuded from him in waves. She knew, he read the sympathy in her soft touch and sad smile, but it wasn't enough.

He'd been here for the last month and needed to see his family. So far, he'd only caught a glance of them from behind the thick, glass wall. Sara hadn't allowed actual touch at that point, and even now, the sight of his mother collapsing in his father's arms haunted him.

"Just give me some kind of timeframe. That's all I need."

She shook her head and released a long, huffing exhalation. "Look, so long as you continue like this, I'd hope within the next two months. Just don't hold me to that. Your body,

organs, and skin are grafting to the metallic skeleton. The biotronic energy pack is now running your circulatory systems well, but needs a little tweaking to stabilize its output. It's like you've been reborn. Your brain is still learning to cope with the altered neural interface."

He hissed, hating hearing the extent of his 'replacements', yet needing to know it all. "I get it. I'm the first to have been able to survive the implantation program physiologically."

"Michael, you're special. This treatment has never before been as successful, and we have to be careful." She touched gloved fingers to his face, her eyes sad while her lips drooped. "Let me be cautious with you. I want you to live. You're just going to have to understand that right now you have a lot of limitations."

He nodded, dissatisfied with her words but clutching the intent close. "Okay, two months. Let's work on that timeframe." It wasn't enough information to settle his frustration, but he could work with that. For now anyway.

"Good. Let's get back to your physio now. Show me your swing."

He moved his arm, dismayed as he always was to realize he didn't have full motion yet. The muscles twanged and ached, the pain increasing the more he pushed. Dots of liquid—*sweat*, his mind added—lined his upper lip and brow.

Sarah reached out and cupped his shoulder lightly. "Stop, Mike. You're pushing too hard."

He bared his teeth, trying harder against the whirling vortex of pain that exploded. "I can do this."

She tugged the racquet from his hand. "Enough." She inhaled as if fighting her own pain. "That's enough for today."

He growled. "I can do more. I should be able to do more. I was a semi-professional athlete and surgeon!" Frustration eked out, and she caressed his cheek.

"I know. But your body has changed. The muscles atrophied and are now healing. They're forming new connections that are fragile. You can't expect to be what you were...yet. It will come. You know that. But right now, let your body heal in its own time."

He subsided, slumping into the seat behind him. Everything she said was true. He knew it, yet none of it made him feel better. If anything, it simply made him realize how he'd never truly grasped the truth when he'd said the same things to his patients.

"You need to rest now, Mike. Settle into your couch and plug in. You'll feel better for it."

Weakness. He hated it, but it hovered constantly, a crow which sat on his shoulder as a reminder. The companion of last choice.

"You've come such a long way in the last couple of weeks, but *you died*. We were able to save you at a cost. You know that. Now you must accept that you're different. Not who and what you were before."

He wasn't who and what he was. *Oh, I bloody well knew that.* It didn't make any of this easier to take though.

The concern that echoed in her voice left him aching. Once, long ago, he'd considered pushing their friendship to more, but now he wasn't even really human. He was both more and less.

His hopes and dreams were shattered. He knew Sara made every attempt to treat him the same as she always had, but they both knew nothing could ever be the same again. He would never be the same. That thought chased him into sleep.

CLARISSA TUGGED AND PULLED, her restraints weakening with creaks and groans. She'd been

here a long time. Long enough for the initial scars to change to a faded pink and her physique to return to what it had been.

Long enough to have counted every panel in the ceiling and for her mind to work up impossible scenarios of escape. How long she couldn't quantify, but long enough that she'd been poked and prodded and felt like an experiment or a lab rat. She'd been spoken of like some kind of creature without a soul or brain. Stripped of her humanity.

"I'm a fighter," she murmured, holding onto the sliver of her soul that hadn't shriveled under the constant torture, because it was all she had left to hope for.

Torture. Her daily treatments and experiments were a torture no one could ever perceive.

The door opened, and she stilled. It wouldn't do to let them know she was fighting her bonds. She'd learned that lesson early on, after they'd sedated her the couple of times they'd caught on to what she was doing.

I won't give in to the loss of control. Her stomach wobbled at the memory of those occasions. And the repercussions that had followed.

"Good morning, Clarissa. We're here for our daily session. Today we're going to test your pain reflexes. See what difference your bio-cybernetic implants have made. It's been a while and we need to see if the settling of the implants has changed the parameters at all. We specifically wish to see if it's affected your ability to cope with cold, heat, and so on. Do be a good girl and cooperate."

Jeremy. He'd been the one that instigated all the previous sessions she'd survived. She hated him.

"I'm not a lab rat." She bit the words out, and he sighed, shook his head, and treated her to one of his signature you've-got-no-idea looks.

"Clarissa, dear. You're so much more to me than a lab rat. I've told you before, you're my crowning achievement. You walk and talk. You think. Just. Like. A. Human."

Clarissa's hair stood on end at his tone of voice. He leaned in, his expression turning feral, and she shrank back from his fetid breath, wondering how she'd ever thought him her friend and future lover.

"But you're not. We saved your life when we operated on you. You should be grateful that I took such an interest in you. If it wasn't for me—"

"I didn't want this. I never asked for it." She hated the desperation in her voice.

For the first time, he looked startled, then a canny look settled on his face. "No, maybe you didn't. But I had the choice. You were the one I saved. Not the others."

His words dropped on her, heavy weights she didn't want. Couldn't welcome. "Others?" He shrugged. "Inconsequential. You were the best choice."

Others. There'd been others? He'd chosen? She struggled to remember what had come before and was left gasping as a lance of pain shifted through her brain. She struggled against the blank wall that surrounded her previous knowledge of herself. She'd tried before, but it was as if someone had walled out that portion of her life. Why couldn't she remember?

"You shouldn't struggle, Clarissa. It's not good for your body or your mind. Now, stay still, I have some students here who are keen to run their tests." He stepped back as two men strode forward, wearing clear glasses she'd come to fear. That meant splatter. Blood or other liquids.

Neither was really young she realized as she gazed into their eyes, noting the way they appeared flat and focused. Looks she'd seen before in other eyes when they only saw a procedure that treated her as inhuman.

"No!" Clarissa screamed. The echo resounded, but no one commented, they simply took their positions beside her strapped gurney.

None cared that she was sentient. Human. To them, she was simply an experiment. Another man trundled in a machine, power cords and long clamps folded across its top, and she shivered. It reminded her of an oversized battery charger. The thought increased the nausea that boiled in her belly, the acidic taste of bile sliding into her mouth. She fought it. Whatever they were going to do wouldn't be pleasant.

Clarissa shuddered and sucked in a deep breath as the man plugged the machine in, extending the cords and leads, then moved around her to fasten bits to the side of her bed.

Should she twist those bonds again? Would that work in her favor? Thoughts and ideas, wilder than before, ran through her brain. *Escape*, her mind screamed. *Don't get caught. Plan.*

"We're charging now, doctor." The one who'd wheeled in the machine advanced with the clamps and settled them on her wrists, while the others unfastened the gown covering her and started attaching probes to her chest, wrists, and head.

The wobble increased and became a full-blown panic attack as they started talking about megahertz and brain patterns. Blackness edged at her mind as she fought to suck in enough oxygen. Each move, every word, only increased her terror.

"Please..." She tried to engage one of them, hoping they'd read the panic and take pity on her, but they didn't gaze at her eyes.

That avoidance left her fearful, not wanting to know their plans, fearing what lay ahead yet strangely accepting of her lot.

———

MICHAEL ROLLED out of the bed. His body strong, his mind clearer than it had been since the accident that had claimed his life. Today was the day Sara was completing his release papers from the hospital. *I'm going home.*

Satisfaction never felt so good, he thought, striding to the window and looking out onto the park opposite his hospital room.

Sara had warned him that his release would come with some restrictions, but he could live with that. After all, he'd sleep in his own bed and be with his family.

The door opened, and he spun around. Sara strode into the room, her brow furrowed, followed by two security officers, their faces tense. Michael's adrenaline surged, but he stayed still, waiting for them to explain this sudden intrusion.

"What's this, Sara?" He indicated to the two men, and she grimaced.

"I told you there would be restrictions. Well, the first one is, because the media got wind of your release, you're going to have security escorts. This is for your safety. We're going to take you down to the VIP entrance, where a car will be waiting. Your father couldn't come, because the house is locked down with paparazzi waiting to get a photo of you." She changed position, shifting to the left, her gaze sliding over his shoulder, and inhaled. "Secondly, you're not going straight home."

He opened his mouth, and she lifted her hand, willing him to settle.

Frustration thrummed, but he waited, barely leashing his furious reaction.

"The powers that be requested we place you in a halfway facility."

His ire rose, face flaming. "Why? I've not done anything—"

"No, Michael, it's not because of you or anything you've done. They...umm... They want you somewhere so they can evaluate your psychiatric status. There's only been a few other cyber-organic transplant patients who survived surgery. None as extensive as you, but none could be released. They didn't cope very well with the changes of their systems. None were able to transition to everyday life. The government needs to be sure of your state of mind."

"You said I was the only one." Fury grew, and he fisted his hands. "I'm not like that anyway. I'm *ready* to go home."

"No, Michael." Her voice firmed. "They didn't know about others until a report was made to the authorities a few weeks ago, but it was kept under wraps given your personal circumstances. I didn't know anything about it until last night when this was presented to me as the only resort. And yes, I agree, you exhibit no negative tendencies, but the authorities need to be sure of the safety and security of the populace."

She advanced, brushing off the concerns of the guards.

"But your current anger won't help, so sit down and listen." She reached for him, even as the two guards thrust their hands to their belts.

He stalked to the bed and dropped down. It dipped and creaked beneath him. His hiss of anger was long, loud, and she winced at his obvious frustration. "Right. I'm listening."

"Good. You're to be released to a halfway facility. Your parents and siblings can visit as often as they like. The added benefit is no one will be mauling you while your body is healing, which, I have to be honest, concerned me."

Michael had to work hard to contain his snarl.

"Your transplants are new, and I don't want you to be physically manhandled and run the risk of infection," she continued. "It's a win—the only one you're going to get. Otherwise, you'll have to stay here until they determine you are emotionally stable enough. You must recognize it's harder here, because the conditions are manufactured. It would take longer to achieve the outcome necessary, and I'm not sure that would be untainted. This way, you'll have freedom to come and go to some degree. Please, understand, I've fought hard for this. For you."

He snorted. "What's the alternative? If I choose to leave and not enter the halfway house or remain here?"

She shuddered and looked away.

Michael frowned. "Sara?"

"You'd be disengaged. That's the only other alternative." Her words were muffled, movements edgy as if she fought some great emotional turmoil.

It took a moment for the words to refine in his mind.

Disengage. Disengage his bio-tronic life support battery? "Sara?" Oxygen clogged in his throat, almost choking the life from him. "They'd do what?"

She reached out, placing her hand over his. "I'm sorry, Michael. You need to understand.

I didn't choose any of this. I know you're exactly as you were mentally, but the psychologists don't. You have to prove to them that you're still human and the Michael we all knew before your accident."

Heavy and dark emotion, the kind he was unused to, coursed within his body. It wasn't anger. Nor was it frustration. Instead, it was some powerful mix—potent and scouring. Fury took the leading edge. He clenched his fists, hiding them behind his back so the guards wouldn't see.

A small monitor, yet another implantation created to assist him in monitoring his emotions and physical status, slid over his vision and showed him the level of distress radiating from him. It not only captured the levels of his breathing, but also that of Sara's increased respiration and perspiration. It reminded him, forcibly, of what he wasn't any longer and the humanity he'd lost.

It took seconds—five point three to be exact—for him to control himself, release the pressure in his hands, and his endorphin levels to begin decreasing. "Then I'll go, Sara. I'm sorry." He spoke clearly, his eyes on the guards, who nodded and stepped back. When he looked at her again, she'd dabbed away the tears that had wavered on her lashes.

This is the last time we'll meet like this, he promised himself. Not even really friends, but never more. He and Sara could never be anything more than doctor and patient, and for him that was more than enough.

If I had known what lay ahead, I don't think I would have wanted them to save me.

He rose and stepped away.

"Michael?"

He stilled, his gaze settled on Sara. "Yes?"

"I'm..." She hiccuped. "I'm sorry." There was a tremble in her voice, but he refused to let it affect him.

"So am I, Sara." Then he turned slowly on his heel and dismissed her.

Chapter 3

Clarissa stood with her back against the wall as she caught sight of herself in the highly polished metal. This was the first time she'd been freed from the bed for as long as she could remember. She looked human, except for the glow of her eyes. The scars, the ones roping her body, ridged though fading to a lighter pink, along with others, the newer ones, were joined with burns and jagged tears. Every one reinforced her status of 'cyber-organic entity'. That's what they'd said she was. Not human. That was long gone.

She didn't know, nor was she able to guess, the duration of her incarceration. Long enough to almost forget her name. "Clar-iss-a." She spoke quietly, afraid they'd hear. Know that the worst of their programming had failed. In the last time period, they'd attempted to even strip that small shred of humanity from her.

They'd coined the name COE for her, expecting her to answer like a lapdog to it. The things they'd done were horrific. Almost as bad as what they'd expected her to do and become.

She blinked, and a tiny trail of moisture escaped, rolling down her cheek. *Tear.* The word came to her, and she frowned. A tear was a human reaction to pain. She wasn't human anymore. They'd reinforced that time and again.

The door opened, and a tech scurried in carrying a tray. One of the few things they attended to now on a daily basis was meals. In the darkness of memory, she remembered the doctor instructing them to ensure she was adequately nourished. *"After all, far too much has been invested for us to fail to keep her in top condition."*

Jeremy. He'd been much more to her once. Now he was her tormentor. The one who'd stripped her of herself, her humanity, and any hope for a future.

The hopelessness weighed down on her like chains around her mind and body. If only she could find a way out. *Freedom.*

Clarissa desperately needed the wind on her face, the scent of the salty ocean. To make her own decisions. To be what she had been before, if only she could remember.

The tech slid the tray on the table and hurried out without a word, fingers tugging on the edges of the door to shut it, but unlike in the past, it didn't latch closed.

It gaped a little, and unsure, Clarissa advanced. "It's probably a trap. The beginning of another one of their sessions."

She stopped, scared and shaking, reached for the brushed metal and touched it. Nothing. No pain radiated. No sharp screams or threats.

She waited a heartbeat, then another.

I could escape.

The thought emboldened her. She reached out again and carefully opened the door a crack. She peered out. No one stood beyond. No guards with whips or electronic prodders.

She made the split-second decision, swung it open, and slid through the opening, scanning left and right. No alarm sounded, no guards came running.

On a deep and desperately shaky breath she padded to the end of the hall and glanced around the corner. Again, no one was there.

Then she ran, helter-skelter, the simple hospital gown fluttering around her as her long legs ate up the distance until she reached the swing doors.

One last set of doors stood between her and the outside world, and she raced to them, shoved them open, and stilled for a second.

She sucked in a deep lungful of clean oxygen. Her feet were bare, the ground pitted with gravel. She checked her surroundings. Grass to the left, then trees, shadowy in the distance.

Nothing would stop her now, she told herself and propelled her body in the direction of the trees. Once she reached them, there'd likely be a fence—electrocuted or other. She'd get through it.

"Freedom." The word spurred her onward. Heart rate pumping in time with the cadence of her steps, she ran, faster and faster, the wind whipping through her hair.

Once in the trees she skidded to a halt. If she stayed at this level, they'd find her. Glancing up showed there were branches, long and heavy, hanging down. She reached and tugged herself up, noting the scratch of uneven bark and not caring.

The sound of a klaxon split the air. "No time now, Clarissa."

She jumped tree to tree, clutching at the branches and trunks as she fled. They swayed with her every move. She'd need to get down soon, otherwise they'd be able to track her far too easily from the air, and those on the ground would be waiting.

Before her, the tree line ended and a large chasm appeared. The rush of water sounded. Clarissa peered over the edge, her stomach roiling at the drop in front of her. She glanced back and sought out those who hunted her, but so far nothing appeared in her vision. Dogs barked and

voices called out to her. Threats echoed. Go back and face whatever they planned or take a chance? Her need to flee won, and Clarissa jumped.

The crash at the bottom wasn't so bad. They'd inured her to pain with their so-called experiments. Her body coped well, if the readout behind her vision could be believed.

A broken rib or two. Some nasty bruises and cuts. They'd heal.

Instead, Clarissa focused on the choppy water which buoyed her and the way it churned. It buffeted her, and more than one wave washed over her face.

I'll tire soon. I need to find a cave or somewhere to shelter.

Her memories rose. Swimming, the movement of arms and legs in water, breathing to the side. *Swim!* No time to consider anything else, she accepted the knowledge, used it, and aimed for the same side, her mind telling her they'd start on the other side. She'd have time to recover the energy expended. Her battery life was extensive according to Jeremy. At least a month with the recent upgrade. Clarissa hoped that was right, but the extra exertion was an unknown equation.

She found a narrow outcropping, rounded it, and saw with consternation there was no cave. She swam on, eyes scanning about, her arms and legs moving in a desperate rhythm. Time passed as she fought the ebb and flow, then there it was. An egress, darkness against the rocks. She arrowed in, tugging and pulling herself along until her feet scraped the bottom of the river floor. She slapped at the waves, gripped the rocks, and dripped her way to the opening. Peering inside showed her it opened much further back than she'd anticipated.

With careful steps she tiptoed inside and followed the line until she was beyond view.

"I need to find somewhere flat, so I can lie down." She might have all the enhancements Jeremy had fitted, but her body still ached to be horizontal for rest.

Who knew how long until she'd be able to find a port and plug in? Whatever rest she could find, she'd accept.

Carefully picking her way to the back of the cave, she found a sandy area, which was mostly clear of debris. She hunkered down, finally allowing her systems to run a full diagnostic.

For the first time she considered that they may have embedded a GPS clip in her receptors. "Is there a tracker?" She spoke aloud, pleased to hear the huskiness from the disuse of her vocal cords had already abated somewhat.

Negative.

She squinted. *Can I even believe that?*

Clarissa fought against the block in her mind, searching deep until she detected a chink to exploit. Pain radiated, but she used it, and there before her were the memories they'd sought to keep from her. The knowledge of her previous life as a nanny. It also answered her query that she didn't know how to check the fittings and systems they'd installed.

"Make a mental note. Find somewhere to run a full diagnostic for GPS and tracker chips. Oh, and algorithms of energy usage and projections of how long until I need to port in."

She ran shaking fingers through her short hair. They'd shorn it again recently, telling her only human women wore their hair long.

Her fingers slid down her body, brushing against the light cotton. She hated the green hospital gown, but it was all she had right now. A naked body—human or cyber-organic—would raise alarm. And yet, she'd be better off without it weighing her down. She reached back, her fingers finding the fastenings and untying them, and she dropped the garment to the ground.

The *drip, drip, drip* in the distance caught her attention, and she dimmed her sight, hoping that would make the illumination from her glowing eyes less visible. It continued, and she cocked her head to the side, listening. Source—water dripping. *Alert Status - nil.*

She released her pent-up breath and leaned back against the wall. In order for the nano- cybernetic implants to repair the damage she'd need to rest. She forced her eyes to shut, set her micro-comp implant to standby and scan alert status, and let herself drop into a doze.

Chapter 4

Michael walked along the path, noting the verdant greenery of the gardens, stopping occasionally to inhale the scents of flowers. Gardenias, roses, and narcissus existed alongside dianthus, honeysuckle, and forget-me-nots. Each beautiful and fragrant. Calming.

His last session with Carlos, the psychologist, had gone well, and he waited for the release he was sure they'd grant this time.

The nurse, Jennifer, hurried toward him. "Michael, I was wondering where you were. You know I need to be aware of your location at all times."

He gifted her with a small smile. "I just wanted to walk among the plants. They're blooming, and I miss the time outside during the sessions."

Jennifer was tall and muscular. A body-builder in her personal time, it seemed they'd hired her for both her skill as a medical personnel and her strength. She sighed. "I know. That's why I thought you'd be out here, but Dr. Aros wanted you to return to your room after the session." She bit her lip, an incongruous sight for the forty-plus-year-old woman, her biceps bulging even against the custom-made uniform. "Come on. Let's get you back to your room. It's refreshment time."

With a sigh, he allowed the woman to tow him back toward the imposing building. For a halfway house, it was well-guarded he thought, not for the first time.

He'd arrived a month ago, angry at the situation that hadn't been his choice, furious with Sara and desperate to see his family. Since then, he'd had many opportunities to discuss his worries with his closest friends and family. He'd come to understand the reason they were allowed such freedom to come and go was dependent on their willingness to talk with Dr. Aros, who was in charge of his psychological profiling.

One by one, their visits had dropped away as life intruded, the urgency blunted and so on. He understood that. At least now he was able to wear his own clothes and had achieved some measure of freedom.

At the door to the building, he stopped and looked over his shoulder. "I wonder what it will look like in winter."

Jennifer cleared her throat. "Hopefully you'll be home by then."

He spun and scanned her face. A bubble of excitement filled his chest, ballooning it so his breathing became more ragged. To go home. To have his life back... That would be wonderful.

It took a full moment for him to find his voice. "I got my release?"

She grimaced and shrugged. "I don't know. I'm just a nurse."

Just like that, as with every other time he'd allowed himself to hope, the crushing wave of resentment flowed. His whole existence depended on their decision.

He let frustration wash away the pleasure, well aware that even this small interaction was being watched and weighed via camera. He restrained the urge to flip the bird, but it was a close- run thing.

He'd learned that early—to allow himself to run through the gamut of sentiment, but to also keep his physical actions under check. Every negative action carried a reaction, and it was usually something he resented bitterly.

"Okay." He headed to his room. It was lush, tastefully furnished, but it was still a prison. One he wanted to escape. Soon.

He settled himself in the deep chair by the television and waited as the young serving girl wheeled in the cart. He'd judged Mariah to be about twenty. She was of mixed race, the Hispanic tone of her skin offset by the striking anglo-saxon blue of her eyes.

"Mr. Michael. I've got your favorites. Bacon and eggs, orange juice, and fresh fruit. The coffee hadn't finished perking yet when I left the kitchen though. I'll go back and grab that for you." She grinned broadly and he returned it.

"Thanks, Mariah. I could do with coffee this morning."

She tugged the tiny folding table out, laid down the cloth, and arranged his dishes before returning to her cart. "Lunch today is veal. Oh, and I see on *Across the Tides*, Eldora is up for a Nobel Peace Prize. I missed yesterday's episode, so I thought I might catch up this morning's work, then join you for it."

Her smile was so bright he couldn't help but laugh. "You know, I never would have watched a soap before my accident. Now I can't seem to get enough."

"My mama said that once they get you in their clutches, it's hard to get them to let you go." With her light words, Mariah trundled her cart from the room, still chortling away.

If only he could be as light-hearted as she was. So young and eager, with her whole life before her. He sighed and picked up the cutlery. He'd never be that easy again. The curse of his cyber implants weighed him down.

Suddenly his hunger abated, leaving him queasy. Food no longer interested him. In fact, the very scent of it invaded his nostrils and he wanted to shove it away.

Dr. Aros just had to release him. Since his arrival Michael had acquiesced to their every request. He'd contained his emotions while they prodded and poked at his psyche, tested his reactions and emotional responses. Surely that had to be enough?

His hand reaching out to push the table away, he stopped at the knock on the door. "Come in."

The door opened soundlessly, and he waited as Dr. Aros entered. Michael made to rise

but the doctor shook his head. "No. Sit down, Michael. I wanted to talk to you before you start packing."

Packing. The word thrilled him, but he contained his reactions. It wouldn't do to jump to the wrong conclusion.

The plump, gray-haired doctor dragged over a chair from the desk and sat down on it, opposite the tray in front of him. Michael waited, well aware that this was how the doctor started every discussion, with the unnerving silent watching.

The slow cadence of his heartbeat increased. "Start packing? Am I going home?"

"Yes, Michael. You've been here long enough for me to determine that you're controlled enough to coexist with society. I'm satisfied that as long as you don't exhibit any violent or startling tendencies, and with the assistance of a monitoring program and ongoing care from a psychologist, that release is the best option for you."

Michael embraced the words deep inside his soul. Yet caution reared its head. More. There had to be more.

"However, before we finalize your release, I am required to warn you that should you show the slightest hint of backsliding, we will do and authorize whatever is necessary to neutralize the threat you potentially cause society. We will be watching. Society will be watching."

Michael sat still, fingers rubbing together as he waited for the rest of Dr. Aros's edict.

"Tomorrow morning a vehicle will collect you from the front door at eight AM. You will present yourself this afternoon for advanced programming and the fitting of monitoring equipment. This is a mandatory part of your release."

"Fine, doctor. I'll present myself this afternoon wherever you deem necessary." It wouldn't do to argue with the man. Indeed, that would be fruitless and possibly result in unwelcome outcomes.

The man stood, pulled the chair back to where it had come from, and smiled. "It's been a pleasure working with you, Michael, and I look forward to our ongoing relationship." With a tiny nod, the doctor left the room, the door shutting quietly behind him.

Chapter 5

Clarissa ran her fingers through the strands of hair falling around her face. Her stomach cramped, as it did much of the time these days. At least she looked almost normal again. Only yesterday she'd filched clothes off a washing line. The size wasn't perfect, but at least now she didn't look like an escapee from a lunatic asylum. The shoes she'd found by the dumpster weren't comfortable, but they'd do the job.

She trotted down the alley. Some would call her paranoid, but she knew better. They were looking for her. Jeremy was out there somewhere, looking to recapture her, and she'd die rather than let that happen!

A sound echoed. It could have been a gunshot, although it was likely a car backfiring. Still, she dropped to the ground, her body quivering. As she fell, Clarissa's shoulder caught on a metal can, dragging it down so she collided with the metal rim. "Ouch!"

The rattle of the lid seemed so loud, and Clarissa winced.

"Hello? Anyone there?" someone called.

The voice from the end of the alley frightened her, and she jack-knifed up, knees already tucked beneath herself as she straightened off the ground. The sound of her breathing rattled her, and she was sure whoever it was could hear her.

Adrenalin surged, and she pumped her legs, heading away from the voice, the shuffling sound of footsteps. Buildings rose on both sides, shutting out the sun, and the cold infiltrated down to her bones, leaving them aching.

Even as she ran though, the sound of pursuit rang in her ears. The more she ran, the less sure she was of her surroundings. She hurried into the street, and early morning walkers parted to allow her past, but she paid them no attention. Getting away and to freedom was her aim.

The further away from the main area of the town she got, the slower she moved, until she settled into a slower gait, hopeful no one would recognize the straggly wraith of a woman.

Ahead lay her lair, the place where she'd found somewhere to hide and recharge. The old, abandoned warehouse suited her needs perfectly. The electrical componentry allowed her to cobble together a connection for recharging her batteries. Now she shared it with another vagrant, though he didn't intrude on her privacy. She'd made that clear when he'd joined her.

Clarissa ducked into the small opening in the door and breathed a sigh of relief.

"Someone see you?" Old Clarrie, a wizened man of indeterminate age, materialized out of the darkness.

"Something like that." She dragged the bag she'd hitched over her shoulder to the ground and rustled around. "This is all I could find. Take what you need."

She dropped a bag of battered cans, a day-old loaf of bread, a couple of boxes of pasta mixes, and turning milk to the floor.

He looked at it and smiled, the gaps between his teeth dark in the half-light. "You did good, kid. But I can look after myself."

He gave a thick, mucus-heavy cough, and she sighed. "You need medical care." "Ain't got no insurance so no medical center for me."

His cough had worsened in the last few days, and fear overcame her. What if he died?

What would she do then? She might have extraordinary strength, but she was a fugitive and a dead body was a giveaway. Too many months spent running and hiding did that to a person, she guessed. It wasn't like she could ask for assistance from her family.

Once, not long after her escape, she'd crept by her parents' house, peering in through the window. The sight before her reinforced that she couldn't return home. Jeremy, the doctor her mother had fawned over before everything happened, sat in the lounge holding her mother's hand, while her father openly cried.

"If only you could have saved her. Doctor, I still can't believe she's gone."

"Mrs. Garrison, you have to let go of your grief. It's been months. I came because your daughter, Diana, contacted me. She explained you were struggling, but to be honest, when Clarissa arrived on my table, there was nothing I could do. No one was as devastated by that as I was in the hospital room. I did everything I could to save her."

She shifted in her seat, nodding. "I know. You're a good boy, and you tried your best. It must have been hard for you too, but you see, it was so quick, then she was whisked away."

His smile was oily, Clarissa thought, watching him from behind the window frame. Practiced. "I know, but it was for the best."

"They wouldn't allow us to view her body. To say goodbye." Her mother's wails shredded her inside.

"No. It was kinder that you remember her as she was."

Clarissa drew back then, unable to stomach any more of Jeremy's lies.

Once she'd considered Jeremy a friend. More so, a prospective mate and possible husband. Instead, the reality proved him a brutal and merciless torturer. Gone was the suave man she'd known. The one who'd squired her to the opera and gallery openings. He'd made her believe that she was the one woman he'd put aside his wealth and privilege to be with.

But she had to put her self-involved thoughts aside and consider the sick man in front of her. It wouldn't do her any favors if the only person she half-trusted now died. "Clarrie, I know you can't see a doctor at the medical center, but if I can get you something to fix that cough, will you take it?"

His gaze narrowed on her. "Don't take any chances, kiddo. I

know you're running from something bad. Old Clarrie can take care of himself." His bravado was ruined by yet another hacking paroxysm.

"Will you take the damned pills if I get them for you?"

He wiped his mouth but not before she caught sight of the scarlet fluid on his hand. "Clarrie? When did that start?" Her stomach bottomed out, cold tendrils snaking through her.

He just shrugged.

She bit her lip, wondering where she might find some assistance. It went against everything she'd learned the hard way, but Clarrie had helped her. She owed him her life after he'd helped her fashion together the power input when it became an urgent need.

He grunted. "There's a clinic on the west side. Free for those on the streets. They know me. If you can get me there, they'll help." His eyes glinted as if daring her, but it was the only opening he'd offered, and she'd gratefully take it.

Wordlessly, Clarissa swooped up and scooped Clarrie into her arms.

"Hey, watcha doing?"

She didn't speak, simply moved toward the door, grabbed one of the old, threadbare blankets from the pile on a box by the exit, and wrapped Clarrie securely. She kept to the shadows, areas where she knew alleys and walkways would allow her an escape route. She'd walked this town for weeks, hunting out the bolt holes and tracks she could use in an emergency.

The cold didn't really bother her. While her skin might goose bump from the cold weather, her pain receptors were so deadened that her skin would almost need to fall off before she'd give in to it. Yet another learning experience she could lay at Jeremy's feet.

Clarissa skirted the main populated areas while Clarrie moaned and grizzled in her arms. When she stopped at the doorstep of the run-down building, she shivered. Her fear of medical personnel rose, a black cloud that terrified her. But she told herself that fear was no reason to let Clarrie die, and he was growing weaker by the day.

Taking a deep breath, she started up the small steps of the old building. She shouldered the door open and carried him in.

"Ma'am? Can I have your name?"

She bit her lip and stood Clarrie up. "It's Clarrie you need to see. Please, he needs a doctor." *Not bad,* she thought. Her voice barely trembled.

The woman squinted over the chipped counter. "Clarrie? Old Clarrie Maycock?"

Clarrie tugged the blanket from around his emaciated frame and nodded. "That's me." Then he coughed, leaving a dribble of blood at the corner of his mouth.

He swiped it away as the woman's eyes opened wide. "Wait here, Clarrie. And heaven help me, if you disappear again..."

"He won't." Clarissa urged the old man into a seat, and she blocked his exit.

The receptionist whirled in a cloud of cotton and bulk.

Clarissa understood and sympathized with Clarrie's urge to flee, noting the way he looked at the door with his muscles tensed. Hers were too, but she controlled herself. He'd purposely hidden from the world just as she did.

"No way, Clarrie. You're here and will see the doctor. I'll wait with you."

The nurse returned. "And you are?" The woman's hand hovered over the card, pencil in hand.

Clarissa frowned. "I'm just a friend."

"Yes, but your name?"

The woman was insistent, and Clarissa coughed. "Alyssa. Lissa." The name they'd agreed she would give if asked rolled easily off her tongue.

"Excellent, Alyssa." The woman's emphasis on her name told Clarissa she hadn't fooled her. Thankfully, lots of unsavory people used this center, so it didn't really matter. "Take a seat, and I'll be right back." The nurse disappeared once again from Clarissa's view.

Clarrie sighed and slumped in the dark, battered, plastic chair but made no attempt to escape, and Clarissa was pleased the waiting room was empty. She didn't want to have to manhandle the older man. One, because she was sure she'd hurt him, and two, because it might tip the nurse or receptionist or even the doctor off to her status.

No, she definitely couldn't allow that.

She pulled her ragged pullover a little closer around her body.

"Come on, Clarrie, the doctor will see you now."

Clarrie stood and shuffled two steps then glanced over his shoulder. "I go, you go." Clarissa gave an inward sigh and followed the man through the maze of curtains to the end of a small hallway. One of the curtains was pulled back, and Clarrie ducked inside. For a second Clarissa considered the distance to the door then groaned. She'd promised, so she entered the cubicle and pasted herself against the wall as the trembling began.

Doctors, hospitals, medical facilities. She'd avoid any she could. Her brain screamed that they were the place of butchers and experimentation.

⬛

THE WOMAN STANDING beside his patient looked bone white. Terrified of him and the whole medical thing, in his opinion.

It appeared to be a common state in this practice. For a moment Michael wondered if she was a prostitute or user—she had the drawn, sunken look he knew well, and her hair looked like a hacked mess. Her frame was thin to the point of skeletal. He noted the way she tugged the worn covering around herself. Clearly though, for all she was here against her better instincts, she was worried enough about Clarrie to bring him in.

The old-fashioned folder, emblazoned with Clarrie's name, felt heavy and full. He opened it and sighed. *Homeless. Great.*

"Hi. You're Clarrie, right? I'm new here and still getting used to everyone, but Vi, the receptionist, said you were coughing blood." He slid into the seat and faced his patient.

The old man shrugged then coughed once again. Michael caught a hint of scarlet and sighed as the old man wiped it away with the none-too-clean back of his hand. Wordlessly, he passed the old man a wipe and gave him a moment to clean up.

"Lissa here insisted I needed a doctor."

He glanced up at the woman who was doing an impression of a statue attempting to blend into the wall.

"He's been coughing for ages and needs medication of some sort." She spoke carefully, as if she'd memorized what needed to be said.

He checked the notes again. On at least three separate occasions the patient had arrived at the clinic with pneumonia, one of which had resulted in hospitalization. He'd had a heavy cough for as long as he'd been attending the clinic. But blood in his sputum was concerning.

"How long has this blood been occurring?"

Clarrie frowned and shrugged, and the woman who'd given the name Alyssa, according to the receptionist with the fake-name look, shook her head. "At least three weeks, maybe longer."

"Any other symptoms?"

She screwed up her face. "He's short of breath. Can't walk far without wheezing and isn't sleeping well."

Michael reached into the drawer and removed a device. He grabbed a tube. "Clarrie, this is called a spirometer. I want to test your lung capacity, okay?"

The old man eyed him with concern. "Why?"

"Because I want to see how much oxygen you're getting and how efficiently you can inhale and exhale. It will help me to work out what's wrong with you." He already had a fair idea but needed to be sure.

He put the unit together, inserted the tube, and ran through a list of questions about smoking, age, and whether he suffered from asthma. To each Clarrie either answered negatively or evaded the question altogether.

"Okay, I'm going to get you to put this peg on your nose, inhale as deeply as you can, then breathe into the tube. We should only need to do this a couple of times."

Clarrie did, and Michael encouraged the man to keep exhaling until he coughed. It was severe, and while he'd gathered a lot of information, it reinforced his concern for the well-being of the man.

"I'm worried, Clarrie. What I'd like to do is run a couple more tests just to make sure we're treating this properly."

Clarrie harrumphed, as if he were about to remonstrate, but Lissa growled. "Let him do his job, Clarrie."

Michael cocked an eye at her. "When I'm done here, if you need assistance, I'm sure we can—"

"No. I don't do doctors and medical stuff. Help him."

Her firm and flat tone made the intention of her words clear. He wouldn't get anywhere with her right now. Funny, she sounded well-educated, and he wouldn't have expected such vehement resistance. She wasn't like the usual by-the-hour client who sought their assistance.

Michael shrugged. She would need to ask for assistance before he offered again. "Right. Clarrie, you need a CT scan. We have a volunteer who's due in tomorrow. I can arrange for her to see you—"

"Don't wanna—"

Lissa reached over and touched the old man's shoulder and he hunched down. "Please, Clarrie. For me. Let's see if we can get to the bottom of what's causing this and get it fixed."

Given the way these two interacted Michael could almost swear this was a father- daughter situation, yet Clarrie had to be in his eighth decade while the woman before him might be twenty or a little older. Certainly, no more than thirty, even with the malnourishment and wild look about her.

"Lissa—"

"Come on, Clarrie. I've nothing better to do tomorrow. You've got no commitments either. I checked with your social secretary." Michael smothered a laugh at her words. "And I can get you here without you needing to walk."

Clarrie sighed and shrugged. "If you say."

She gave a tiny smile and nod. That single action amazed Michael at the change it wrought in her looks.

"For now, Clarrie, I'm going to give you some antibiotics. Something to help clear up the cough, along with a light analgesic. This isn't for sharing."

Clarrie gave a tight laugh. "No one to give it to, and Lissa don't take nothin' like that."

Michael stood, dragged a key from his pocket, and opened the door to the small pharmacy cabinet. They didn't keep a lot of stock on hand, because security in these parts was too much to ask for. What they had was donated by the pharmaceutical companies for testing, or because its due date was looming and they couldn't sell them.

He scanned the offerings and picked one out. "You take this three times a day with food."

Aware of how sore the older man's chest must be, he pulled out some light analgesics, giving instructions for their use, then closed and locked the doors. "You need to stay as warm and dry as possible."

"I'll make sure that happens, doctor." Lissa pushed away from the wall as he thrust the packs of tablets into the old man's hand.

"I'm sure you will. If you'll wait in the front area, I'll arrange his appointment for tomorrow morning."

They left him then and he frowned. Something in the woman's gait—stiff, as if trying to get used to prosthetics—set off alarms in his mind.

He picked up the phone and tapped out reception's number. "Can you arrange for Clarrie to meet with Tam tomorrow morning? He needs a CT scan. Run him through the procedures too. And I'll want a follow-up appointment as soon as possible."

"Sure will, doc." The line went dead.

Michael sat there, rapping his fingers on the desk long after he was sure they'd left.

***

CLARISSA SETTLED Clarrie on his pallet, checked to make sure he was warm, and went to board up the entry to the warehouse. It wasn't much, but at least they could be secure here. Since finding this spot, she'd learned that what one had, others wanted. That's how she'd met Clarrie, when he'd hobbled in just days after she'd found the location.

The tug of exhaustion meant she'd need to plug in, but her mind spun in circles, thinking over what she'd done. The chances she was taking in caring for the old man.

"Clarrie isn't your greatest concern." Since Jeremy's work, she'd taken to talking to herself; it had become an integral part of reminding herself of her humanity.

Clarrie knew her secret. He'd found her, port open as she struggled to fashion the necessary cord so she could refresh her batteries. She'd been defeated and ready to give in when he'd staggered over the threshold, late one evening, just as the weather started turning cold.

A sound echoed, a shuffle, and she looked up in time to see an old man, his eyes widening as he scanned the scene before him. Her ragged clothes, the small cover of synthaderm wide open while an electrical cable made connection with her leg.

Her eyes glowed, and she dimmed them with a thought.

He swallowed, and the sickly stench of vomit filled the air.

"Who are you?" Clarissa made to wrench the power connector from her leg. "You're one of those bio-cyborgy things, ain't you?"

"Maybe." She bit her lip.

Her hand grasped the gnarled end and the end she'd finally found that matched the

portal opening in her leg. Why Jeremy had chosen there for her plug-in she'd never know. But it wasn't as if she intended to ask him.

"You know what you're doing?" the old man asked, and she shrugged.

He tugged the cord and ending, squinted, and reached beyond her for the tools she'd found. In a few short, quiet minutes, he'd fashioned what she needed and shoved it at her.

"Uh, geez, that buzzes a little." She shunted the port into the opening, watching him closely.

If he ran, she'd have to unplug and either chase him or find somewhere else to stay. The idea of finding another place with similar facilities—somewhere to fuel up her battery—didn't appeal, especially as she'd allowed it to run low.

"I heard about yous. They were showing them on the television when I went past the store. Reckon they're dangerous. You don't look too dangerous right now." The old man leaned on the doorframe and gave a rattling cough.

"Maybe. Maybe not. But you look like you need somewhere to stay. You thinking on making this that place?" She tensed, wondering if this was the best course of action, yet unwilling to let him go.

Perhaps it was a shadow of her caring instinct. After all, she'd been a nanny before her life went so radically wrong.

"If you could spare a corner, I wouldn't cause you no harm." He coughed again and Clarissa made a split-second decision.

"Stay here. There's plenty of room. Just don't bring anyone else and you'll be fine, okay?"

He nodded, but remained still, watching. "You juicing up?"

She closed her eyes, breathing deeply and banishing the scroll of the info screen. "Yeah, it's working. Thanks. Look, I'm not up for talking. Find yourself a corner, make up a bed, and settle down for the night."

She waited until the shuffle faded away, waited for him to settle while she forced the beat of her heart to slow to its usual rhythm.

That had been months ago. Since then she'd bonded with the old man. She cared about him and had an inkling he felt the same.

Clarissa checked to ensure the door and windows were closed, and then found her plug-in port where she'd stashed them. Most of the itinerants around here knew this as her place, but someone new, on the hunt for something to sell, might stumble across her flop. She couldn't afford to replace the cords, so she kept them stashed in a hidey-hole in the center of the building.

She also realized that once the cold weather passed, she'd need to move on. Find another refuge. Maybe she could raise some cash, purchase an ID so she could find employment. Clarrie might even...

"No. He can't come with me." In all likelihood, he'd be dead by the end of winter. It wouldn't be a stretch, given how ill he seemed. Pain speared her even as she considered the possibility, but reality couldn't be ignored. She was running for her life, and being burdened by an ill man would only make things harder. Of course, if he lived and got better... She blanked that out. "You can think on that later."

Instead, she thought back to the man at the clinic. The way he'd moved had been odd. Jerky. And his face was lined as if by recent pain. She knew that well. It was her reality.

Clarissa rubbed at one of the connective scars that ringed her limbs. They'd replaced sections of bone with titanium, and connected the tissues with enhanced filaments. She knew pain really well.

"Come on. You need to settle in, 'cause Clarrie needs to be back at the clinic in the morning." So, she retreated to the small bed she'd made from flattened cardboard boxes, and the blankets she'd been given by the charity people. It wasn't much, but it was better than the cave she'd started out in.

Her stomach cramped. She'd need food in the morning, and she remembered the stash she'd picked up before seeing the blood. Better to leave it until morning. Clarrie would be hungry by then, and she could hold on. She'd learned how to.

Instead, in her mind, she focused on green fields, waving sunflowers, and let the warmth of her imagination grow deep inside.

Chapter 6

Michael waited, unsure if Clarrie and the girl, Lissa, would arrive. Something about her tugged at him, as though they were joined by an indefinable connection. How that could be eluded him. After all, she was homeless. He wasn't. He was now a bio-cybernetically enhanced human. She wasn't. She was likely a prostitute or drug user. He wasn't.

Most people might distrust him if they knew what he was, but it seemed she trusted no one.

He laughed at the stupidity of his thoughts. She'd already brushed off his concern, and he wasn't one to take further chances. Instead, he tapped at the computer, checking the report he'd put together, brief though it was. The indications from the scan told the story of Clarrie's suffering.

He could see the long-term scarring on the old man's lungs. Michael breathed out heavily. It looked like bronchiectasis to him. Not the most severe form, and while Clarrie didn't have a case of pneumonia, unless he started to care for himself it could end up with a visit to the emergency ward.

Michael pressed the buzzer on his desk, and that large nurse who'd been on duty the night before stuck her head around the corner.

"You rang?"

He grinned at her dry words. "Mary, can you contact the drug store? I need to place an order for some stronger antibiotics. Plus, I want to set up a couple more repeat appointments with Clarrie."

"Sure, but whether he comes back or not..." She shrugged. "He's a bit of a pain to get back here once he's got an initial course. We've had a lot of problems with that in the past."

"Do what you can then. Oh, and the girl with him, Lissa?"

"Never seen her before, but judging by the looks of her, I'd say she's been living rough for a while." Mary entered the room and dropped into the visitor's seat where Clarrie had sat the night before. "I've never seen her around before. You get to know the locals after a while. She's new. But there's something about her, doc. Reminds me of a wounded animal."

He nodded. "I know. When Clarrie comes in, can you try and engage her in conversation? Find out—"

She shook her head. "You know as well as I do, unless she wants help, you're not going to get anywhere. I see this every time, doc. It's rare they accept help on the first or even second go round. But I like you. You've turned up every day for a week, taken the worst shifts, and are doing it for free. In my books, that makes you all right. So, I'll try." She lifted her ample bulk from the seat. "Now, Mrs. Murphy is out there waiting to see you. She's one of the ongoing patients, presenting with her usual range of symptoms."

Mary thrust the folder into his hands, and he opened it, scanned the information. "Okay, send her in."

As Mary left, he cast a final glance at Clarrie's file. He'd get back to that soon enough.

▭

CLARRIE WOKE and Clarissa was ready, milk in hand and one of the heat-up foods in a battered pan she'd scared up. "Come on, Clarrie, you need to eat."

He grumbled but complied. She watched him like a hawk until the food was gone. "You eaten yet?"

"Yeah." She'd managed a couple of slices of bread and some milk. It would keep her going, but right now, Clarrie was the one who needed good nourishment. Warm clothes. She sighed. Beggars certainly couldn't be choosers.

Not that she felt great. There was a greasy overlay of heat in her body, and her stomach ached viciously.

The cold and the poor food, she theorized. Clarrie was the one who was sickest though, so she ignored what ailed her and continued to care for the older man the only way she knew how.

She twisted the caps off the bottles, dropped one of each of the pills into her cupped palm, and handed them to him. Then she waited to make sure he took them.

"We're going to have to move, Clarrie. You have to get to the clinic, and I don't want you running late."

He pushed up, groaning and grunting. "You're just like my ex-wife. She used to poke and prod too. Cut from the same damned cloth."

Clarissa smiled. It was the first time he'd spoken about family, so clearly, he was either getting used to her or she was getting on his nerves. Whichever it was, the outcome remained the same. Positive.

"Come on. Let's get you moving. I managed to find some cleaner clothes and put them in the old bathroom. You go along and get cleaned up while I clear away."

As Clarrie hobbled off, she set about washing the pot in the small dish of water in what had been the staff lunch room, then hurried back to her corner, tugging on the old jumper she'd worn yesterday. Clarrie was used to the scars now, but she had no intention of baring them for the world to see. That would just be inviting more problems.

She ran her fingers through her ragged hair and wished silently that she could once again have her long, golden hair back. Now it just looked greasy and limp. Uneven from where she'd sheared off the hanks with a sharp knife.

A warm bath wouldn't go astray either. Instead, she had to make do with the chipped sink of the bathroom. Better than most of the homeless though, she conceded.

Clarrie opened the door, and she marched up to him, examining his face, and smiled. "Good. Let's get out of here."

At the doorway, she tugged off the board that she used as a lock and shoved it to the side. She cracked the door open and peered out. A car, black and gleaming, drove slowly past the building, and she shrank back. She'd know that vehicle anywhere, the driver sealed away from his passenger with a plasglass screen.

"OhmyGod." She couldn't stop the words from escaping. *Jeremy.* She slid the door shut.

"What's up?" Clarrie came up behind her and tried to open the door, but she kept it firmly closed.

"Not yet." Bile rose, and the cold seeped inside her skin, freezing her belly.

"Lissa?" Clarrie slid his hand onto her shoulder.

"It's him. Jeremy. They've just driven by."

Had he found her? If so, how? She'd been careful, kept an eye out. Thoughts and ideas rolled in her mind. She'd have to move on, find another location. Somewhere away from the city. "Let me check." Clarrie's voice sounded like it rang from a distance, and she started, realizing she'd been lost in her fear.

"I'm going to have to leave, Clarrie." Her voice wobbled, and for the first time since finding this location, she felt abject fear.

"Let's wait and see what he—"

"But if he's found me—" The thin edge of panic colored her tones.

"And we don't know if he has. Calm down, girl. He's probably looking for you but doesn't have a clue how close he's come." Steel ran through his words, and she stopped speaking, swallowed, and nodded. Of course, Clarrie was probably right. It didn't make her feel any better though. Jeremy had been so close, and if she hadn't been as cautious...

"You're right. But just to be safe, we'll give it a couple of minutes before I check out there again."

She stood still, waited until the internal screen inside her skull told her ten minutes had passed. With a thought, Clarissa activated the intense hearing part of her programming chip and cracked the door open. She waited and scanned, watching for any sign of movement.

Satisfied no one was watching, she silently indicated to Clarrie with a wave of her hand, and together they left the building. She'd scouted out the area extensively, so she knew many of the alternative laneways and kept to them, shuffling slowly so Clarrie, who insisted he already felt a lot better, could keep up.

While Jeremy had money—being a certified billionaire as he'd skited one night during an intimate dinner for two—and genius ranking on his side, along with a bunch of burly guards, she had caution and a newfound sneakiness to rely on. They had kept her safe thus far.

The tension that had built up within her finally ebbed away as she reached the door to the free clinic. Silently, she shoved the door open and stepped inside.

MICHAEL WASN'T sure what the commotion was that echoed from the front, but he shoved away from his seat and hurried to the reception area.

Clarrie sat hunched in a chair, holding the hand of Alyssa, who crouched in front of him, while Mary bustled about.

"Drink some water, girl. Then I'll get the doc to see you."

"I don't need to see a doctor. Clarrie is the one who needs him."

Mary clucked and fussed while Michael watched the tableau unfolding before him.

Clarrie, his patient, was patting Alyssa's hand. "You need to see the doc too. You don't go, I won't."

Michael grinned at the air of fragility that the old man assumed. "Did I hear someone call for me?"

All three heads jerked in his direction, and for a moment he found himself lost in the pale blue of Lissa's gaze. "I don't need to see you."

"Don't be stupid, girl. You nearly passed out, and if I don't miss my guess, you haven't got any cash or medical insurance either. And Old Clarrie here said he won't see the doc if you don't see him too."

Her lips thinned, cold slits of pale flesh. Her eyes narrowed too, and Michael was sure he felt the icy chill of winter in her gaze.

Michael advanced. "I'll take a look and won't pass judgement on anything except your medical state, I promise." He kept his words light and a little teasing.

Clarrie rose. "Come on, girl. You pushed me into coming here, now it's your turn." "You know why, Clarrie," she hissed. "Don't do this to me."

"'Bout time someone did. Now cut rope." With that he stumped toward Michael. "I'm here because I promised I'd see you." Then the old man stamped down the corridor to the curtained cubicle.

Michael turned to Mary. "Don't let her go." Then he followed Clarrie down the hall.

━━━

CLARISSA SEETHED. She felt a little unwell, it was true, but she couldn't afford to be caught up with a doctor. He might know Jeremy, and then she'd be in more danger than ever before. A situation she just couldn't allow to happen.

But even as she tried to push up out of the seat, five-foot-nothing of bulk loomed, and a wave of vertigo hit her.

"Where do you think you're going?"

She sighed. Clarissa knew, for now, she was beat, and she settled back in her seat. "Nowhere," she mumbled.

"Good. Now be a good girl and wait for the doc."

She waited, knowing that Clarrie was seeing the doctor by himself. Would he be okay? Only time would tell.

When he came stumping down the corridor she sat up. "Everything okay?"

"I'll be fine, girly. I need to talk to Mary over here though, and the doc said you're to go on through."

Something must have shown on her face as he gave the you-go-

or-else stare, and she headed up the corridor. When she arrived, the doctor was waiting and indicated the seat, which she sat in with a heavy sigh.

He drew the curtain and stood in front of her. "So, what happened out there?"

She shrugged, wondering if she assumed a teenage attitude, he might leave her be. "Don't be childish. What symptoms are you presenting?"

She blinked at hearing the frustration in his voice. So much for that working.

"A little dizziness, some temperature fluctuations."

He cocked his head at her words. "Sore throat? How bad are the temps?"

She swallowed. "My throat's good. A bit of spiking, but you know, it's winter coming."

"And you're living rough?"

"Not by choice." She couldn't stop the mutter then sighed. *I really need to learn to keep my mouth shut.*

The doctor scooped up his stethoscope. "Jumper off so I can listen to your chest."

Now terror erupted. "No."

He stood firm, looming over her, and her vision narrowed. "Jumper off or—"

A mixture of terror and fury pushed her to surge off the chair. "I'm not going to let you touch me."

"Who hurt you, Lissa? Who frightened you so much that you'd fight against this? All I want to do is help you."

The gentleness in his words stopped her. Destroyed her. Tears welled, hot and unbidden, then traced down her cheeks.

"Please, don't." She reached out, felt him grip her fingers. "Please."

What she was asking for, she honestly didn't know. It wasn't for pity.

"Sit down and let me help you."

She desperately needed someone to be kind to her, but it might break her once and for all, into tiny pieces. Then if Jeremy found her...

Clarissa cleared her throat. "I really need to go."

"You really need to stay. Lissa, if this is something that can be fixed, I'll help you."

Her stomach rumbled with hunger, and she sighed. "You can't."

"You might be surprised. Let me try."

His eyes glinted, and she narrowed hers, wondering if she was more sick than she thought. For a second, she was sure—

"What—who are you?"

His lips, wide and generous, flattened at her words. "What am I? I'm a doctor. Did you expect something different?"

She shook her head, and another wave of nausea and dizziness hit her. She reached out as blackness crept into the corners of her mind. The clouds that threatened her crowded in until she could only see a pinprick.

With a sigh, she dropped like a stone into the blackness.

MICHAEL CAUGHT Lissa as she slid forward. She didn't seem as boneless though as most others he dealt with. Without effort he hoisted her onto the bed behind him.

He debated calling on Mary, but something told him Lissa wouldn't thank him for involving someone else.

Instead, he checked her temperature and frowned at the spike on the thermometer readout. With a sigh he sat back down and waited for her to come around, which she did in short order.

"Jumper off and let me check your chest."

Obviously, she was surprised and followed his instruction without thought, but stilled once it was off.

"You tricked me."

Her tone was caustic, but he saw the scarring. The marks. "Who did this to you?"

Fury zipped along his veins as he stepped closer, reaching out, but she drew away, and he knew then exactly what had happened.

"Who? Who did this?" he asked again.

Surely it couldn't be Sara? But who else was involved in the bio-cybernetic treatment field? He wracked his brain, but he'd been too long in the medicine wilderness, and Sara hadn't been keen on discussing contemporary medical technologies with him since the accident.

"It's not what you think. I was in an accident."

He pinned her with his stare. "They gave you cybernetic treatments, didn't they?" She shook, and he balled his fists, aware that anything more right now would see her running. "Is that why you're scared? Who did this to you, Lissa? Why?"

He needed to know it all, why she was so terrified and who chased her.

"I can't—"

She breathed deeply, in and out, speeding up, and he reached out with a gentle hand, the action belying his words, but he stilled his hand just inches from her skin. "Bullshit! Tell me, Lissa, 'cause you're so scared I can practically see the terror oozing out of your pores."

She let loose a tiny sob, and he felt like a heel, pushing and prodding, but he couldn't help her until she told him everything.

"I understand, you know," he said gently.

Her head snapped up, her eyes zeroed on his and a sneer gracing her lips. "Like hell!" Until she knew about him, she wouldn't trust a word he said. "I do. Because I've had the

treatment too." He tugged at the buttons on his sleeves and rolled them up, watching as her eyes glazed with shock.

"But...they let you go?"

Her words told him so much. He sighed. "They did. But only because the researcher who worked on me helped me. Gave me chances to remake my life."

Once more her lips wobbled. "They wanted me for a guinea pig. He...he never wanted me, only my body."

He. Clearly not Sara then. Michael breathed deeply, thankful that his old friend wasn't involved.

"Tell me who and I'll try to help you."

"But he nearly found me this morning. He'll take me back and do more experiments. I can't—" The breath she sucked in whistled as her chest heaved. "I won't let him do that to me again. I'm a person. *I feel.*"

Fury rose, scouring his guts. Whoever had done this to her had taken it much too far. The fear, the scarring. And as he inspected closer, he noted not just the therapy scars, but countless other scars that he couldn't associate with any therapeutic treatment.

Ones that looked like healed burns and slices. Not deep enough to damage the layers of nano-cording that replaced sinews or muscle, but enough that the dermal layers would have taken extensive healing. The white slashes, far too precise, could only be knife cuts. The discovery soured his stomach, bile rising, and he fought the nausea back for long seconds.

"Lissa, I know you don't know me. Not really. But would you trust me if I said I know someone who could and would help you?"

She bit her lip and shook her head.

He sighed. "Lissa, the woman who operated on me is a friend of mine. I trust her. She'll help you too, if you let her."

Lissa glanced at him, hope clearly warring with terror.

"Please. Let me take you to Sara. She's... I've known her for years. She's a researcher now with the BioDermal Institute. She's good. Honest. She saved me with this treatment. Let her save you too."

"Clarrie?"

He grunted and decided he'd pay himself for the old man's treatment if that's what it took to get this woman off the streets and into a safe situation. "We'll take him with us. I can get him a bed somewhere and make sure he gets the treatment he needs, but right now, it's you who worries me."

"I don't want him to find me." That whisper came close to undoing him. "Where I'm taking you, you'll be safe. Trust me, I'm a doctor."

Her tiny laugh warmed him.

"Please, Lissa?"

She reached out a hand and took his.

Chapter 7

Clarissa didn't know why she trusted this doctor, but she did. He'd shared that he too had received similar treatment. He'd shown her his scars. They weren't ropey and dark like hers, but careful lines and pucker marks from needle and thread. He'd been so insistent, and she'd been unable to resist. When she'd asked about the spark she'd seen in his eyes, he told her it was the glint of his implants.

Now she sat in the car with Clarrie, as the doctor drove, hoping like hell they didn't pass Jeremy and he wouldn't see her. He'd be looking for her still, and where better to start than a hospital?

The road the doctor had taken out of town was winding, and the sides of the road were dotted with large bushes. The sky darkened as they drove. He turned on the lights, and she watched as the light broke through the gloom.

"Where are we going?"

"The institute has an agreement with a small, private hospital up in the hills. It's where they took me after my accident. That's where I received my treatment. I stayed there until I transferred to a specialist halfway house."

She grunted.

"When they did this to you, where did they take you? It wasn't this hospital."

She knew he was fishing for information, but she'd hedge her bets, not let him know who and where until she was sure of her safety. As it was, she'd only agreed because of her weakness. Clarissa considered his question, then answered. "I don't know where I was. It was near a cliff, but a long way from home. A long way from here. It took a while to find my way here. I hitchhiked after I'd hidden for a couple of weeks. I couldn't... If I'd gone home, he would have found me. As it was, when I got there, he was in the house with my parents. I realized they thought I was dead, and it seemed best to let them continue thinking that."

"Why?"

"Because they were so worried and Je... He knew them. I'd been dating him."

She glanced out the window, hoping to shutdown the conversation. It hurt too much to consider just how gullible she'd been. Jeremy used her. Abused her. "Okay, so then you headed to town?"

She shook her head. "I'm not from around here. I made my way here after I realized that even if I wanted to go home, it wouldn't be safe. Without money, identification, or clothes, there wasn't much choice really. So, I found a location where I could hide out. Then Clarrie turned up on the doorstep, so to speak."

"Judging by the way you talk, you're well-educated. Where?"

She swallowed. "St. Gertrude's, then later on Halmut School for Nannies."

"Really? I know some people..."

She shifted in her seat, deathly afraid that she'd made yet another wrong decision, just one more of so many, and she cursed her loose tongue.

"This friend of yours, she's good?"

"Sara's great. Known her since med school." His tone told her he thought more of her than just as a friend though.

"You're involved?"

"What?" He laughed off her words. "No. I might have considered it a long time ago, but I realized she and I are too different.

She's married to her career. Don't get me wrong. She's a great girl, but I discovered I wanted a family. At least until this." He sighed, and Clarissa found herself fascinated.

"Why 'until this'? I mean, it's not like you can't do things like reproduce." The words emerged like a croak from her throat, but he seemed so sad and lost for a moment that she couldn't help the emotions that welled.

"They were unsure that... Hang on, how do you know that?"

She blinked at the memories. "Look, I really don't want to talk about it, okay? Actually, I think I might have a sleep now."

She turned on her side and closed her eyes, but the reality and memories kept pounding at her. The things they'd done. The experiments.

MICHAEL DROVE, hands clutching at the steering wheel, white and death-grip like. She knew things, had been the subject of experiments, and it left him sickened.

They'd learned nothing since the onset of the Human Production Bill of 2140. All experimentation like that on human subjects was strictly forbidden, and Sara's work, while accepted generally in medical circles, still warred for wider support in the public theatre.

Whatever they've done to Lissa, they will have to pay for it, he thought. He'd talk to Sara, find out who else was working in this area, then he'd call in favors he'd never expected to use.

The ride continued in silence, Clarrie frowning as he sat in the seat beside Michael. Every now and again, Michael would check the rearview mirror, see that Lissa remained still, but his awareness of her told him she wasn't asleep, just ignoring him.

That was okay, because likely before he'd brought whoever had done this to her to justice, she'd probably hate him. He'd need to know it all, find Jonah and Franklin and enlist their help. His buddies had served with him in the GMC—General Medical Corps —during the war of 2142.

Now he'd call in those favors. Six years wasn't too long to wait. It was just right, and he knew exactly what he needed them to do.

They'd bring the animal that caused all this to justice. They had to.

The gates loomed, and he slowed, pulled up to the security gates, and waited for the guard to reach his side of the vehicle. He dropped the window and flashed his ID. "Dr. Sara Windhower is expecting me and two patients."

The guard checked his hand-held device and nodded. "Head on up to the main building. You'll be met at the door."

Michael drove the vehicle slowly, creeping up the long driveway, until they reached the parking area for the main hospital building and waited as Lissa sat up in her seat. "We're here?"

"Yeah. So come on, and Clarrie too. The sooner we get Clarrie settled and into the system, the sooner we can start sorting out what needs to be done for you."

She grimaced and unclicked her safety belt. "Fine. But if he finds me, it's on your head." He winced at the resigned tone.

With her ungracious comment ringing loudly, she opened the door and stepped out of the car.

"Girl has a lot of demons, doc. Give her time. She'll come good. She's better than what you're seeing right now. She's got a good heart."

It was exactly what he thought as they climbed from the vehicle. He avoided any thoughts of the emotions that welled in him every time he looked at her and considered what had happened. If he gave in to that, he'd probably be on the floor throwing a screaming tantrum. That wouldn't help anyone.

Instead, he indicated to the doorway and ushered the two of them forward, hoping he'd made the right decision all around.

Chapter 8

Clarissa sat on the bed, waiting for Sara, the friend of Dr. Michael as he called himself. If she were brutally honest, she had no expectations that anything positive would happen. Only that Jeremy would find her. Before that happened, she'd have to make preparations. She wasn't going to face torture again.

The door opened, and a woman entered the room. Small and compact with dark hair and chocolate brown eyes, the sight made Clarissa feel even less comfortable with her surroundings and situation.

"You're Lissa?"

The woman advanced toward her, and Clarissa nodded.

"I'm Sara. Michael asked if I'd take a look at your scars and get some idea what the situation is with your treatment."

She moved forward, and Clarissa couldn't help pulling back from the woman. The churn of fear ate at her belly. "That's all?"

"Yes. Why would I do anything else?" When her voice remained calm, Clarissa allowed herself a moment to settle her emotions. The woman seemed taken aback by Clarissa's question, and Clarissa sighed.

She'd seen exactly how some behaved given the opportunity to do wrong, but while she questioned this woman's motives, she also knew there were few to no options.

"Just because," Clarissa muttered as she shrugged.

The doctor frowned. "As a researcher and surgeon, I have signed the 'No Harm' oath. I won't hurt you."

The spurt of disbelief erupted. "Sure."

"Lissa, if I were to know the name of the person who did this to you, who hurt you—"

"You'd what? Protect me? Make it all better?" Cold fury warred with sarcasm in her voice, shooting like frozen barbs from her mouth. "You can't. He's too powerful. Has the ability to reach where I don't think even you could stop him."

Sara growled. "You'd be amazed to know who we can call on. The lengths we can go to, ensuring we stop this person. Whoever they are, they aren't beyond the reach of justice."

"You keep believing that, doc. So, are you going to start your examination, or shall I just wait to die?"

The woman started, and a tiny hit of satisfaction filled Clarissa as Sara dragged her stethoscope from around her neck. "Shirt off and lean forward."

Clarissa complied. Nudity was something she'd come to terms with since Jeremy's experimentation. Then she'd learned to escape within herself, to remove her mind from the reality of where she was, and into a place he couldn't ever reach. The place where one man would hold her, love her, and ignore what she was. What had been done to her.

Clarissa tugged off the old, stained jumper, revealing the holed t-shirt below.

"That too."

Clarissa glanced at Sara who'd paled at the sight of her clothing. She shrugged the t-shirt off as well, her entire torso revealed to Sara who sucked in a deep breath. "Who did this to you?"

"He was a doctor." She glanced at Sara and watched as the horror dawned on her face at the sight of the knife marks and burn scars, healed but obvious in their jaggedness.

"No. No doctor would do this. Only a butcher." Sara held her hands to her mouth as if holding in nausea or shock.

"He was. He did all this and allowed others to as well. You seem shocked. Why?" Clarissa leaned forward, well aware of the mass of scars that covered her body. The worst one though, that was hidden from view and in her mind.

"Because we don't harm those who need our care. Whoever he was, he mustn't be allowed to get away with this. It's one thing to slice through human flesh to save a life, but no one has the right to make someone else suffer as you clearly did."

Clarissa cocked her head. "You believe that?" Clearly, Sara had never come across the results of such experimentation, yet Clarissa knew it happened. She couldn't explain the scarring of feeling so damned afraid and alone. "It's not indicative of your reality though, is it?"

"No, Lissa. It's not reality. It might be what he made you believe, but it's not how we, as researchers, think or act."

Clarissa shifted on the examination table. "Look, there were more than enough researchers who joined him. They did this as much as he did. There must have been at least a dozen others. You might get one, you might get two, but I doubt you'll get them all." Pressure built in her chest. "If you're done, I want to get dressed."

"Not yet. I need some vision of these markings."

"No." Now Clarissa tried to shuffle forward as if to stand, but Sara's hand touched her. "Don't touch me." She scurried back.

"I wasn't going to—"

"I said, don't touch me." Her voice rose, tight and panicked, and the door swung open. Michael strode inside the room. "What the...hell."

He stared at Clarissa, revulsion coloring his features. "I'll kill him. Tell me who and—"

Clarissa scooped up the old jumper and pressed it against her scarred chest, but it didn't stop him. Michael came closer, advancing step by definite step. "Let me see," he said.

Her stomach quivered. "No."

"Please, Lissa. I want to help you."

Unlike her reaction to Sara, tears welled and she shook her head, suddenly lost for words.

This strong man wanted to help her, but she couldn't rely on him. If she let someone bolster her, she wasn't sure she'd ever be able to withstand the assault of memories again.

When he reached out, his hand curving over her shoulder, the warmth filled the iciness that had invaded her soul. Then she melted, leaned in as he slid his hands around her, hugging her close.

She didn't stop to think, to consider his actions. Instead, she welcomed his reassurance and support.

"Michael. You can't be in here." Sara's voice echoed in her mind, breaking the connection between the two of them, and while he only drew back an inch, she slammed back into place the barriers she'd erected around herself.

Clarissa refused to meet his eyes, even though the burn of his gaze scorched her.

"I'm not leaving, Sara. Not unless Lissa asks me to."

She opened her mouth, tried to tell him to leave, yet no sound escaped.

"Lissa, do you want him to leave?" Sara prodded, and she couldn't bring herself to shake

her head, even though she knew it would mean Sara would eject him. "Fine then. Take the seat in the corner and don't say a word."

⸺

MICHAEL HAD NEVER BEFORE FELT the scouring of emotions he did now as he watched Sara check Lissa. So many questions warred with the fury. Who was responsible? Could he bring them to justice? Would Lissa ever trust someone again?

None of them were answerable right now.

The one thing he did know was that Lissa had been tortured, raped—whether physically or not, it was too soon to tell, based on the answers she was giving Sara, but physically abused.

"Lissa, have you ever been pregnant? Carried a child?"

Lissa paled and glanced away.

Incandescent rage bloomed, but he controlled his anger with a fair degree of difficulty.

He'd seen that look before and knew what it meant. They'd seen the victims of the war, those who'd been sexually abused.

At the end of the examination, Michael felt like he'd been through the wringer, and that couldn't even begin to describe how Lissa must have been feeling.

"Michael, I can't release her right now. She's malnourished, her body requires a lot of work to build her up. I'm also not sure the nanotech injections she'd received were totally successful. I've got some other tests I want to run."

Lissa growled. "I'm not a test subject. Talk to me, not him."

Michael silently cheered her for the bravado, but knew it was tissue thin. "I'd have to agree. But if you admit her, I stay too."

"What? I thought you couldn't wait to get away before?" Sara's words teased him, yet he heard the underlying question: Is this woman important to you?

It was a question he couldn't answer. So, he didn't. All he knew was if he left her here, she'd most likely be gone by the time he returned.

He stayed close by, not speaking unless Lissa asked for his input, and watched her, amazed at the strength this fragile and damaged woman exuded. He'd seen the fear in her eyes when Sara initially stated she wanted to admit Lissa to the hospital, her muscles tensing until he suggested the halfway house where he'd continued his recovery on the far end of the grounds.

The transfer took place in total silence, and it allowed him to think over and brood on what he'd learned. He'd need to make contact with his compatriots soon.

Lissa hadn't been happy until they'd arrived and she'd been able to inspect the room they assigned her. Once she was admitted, he requested the room he'd vacated months ago, thankful that this section of the hospital was so far removed from any other patient or treatment suites.

Her room was next to his, and he'd shown her how close he was.

"Where's Clarrie?" Her voice husky from hours of questions and answers, fear and frustration, he surmised.

"He's going to need more advanced care. He's at the main hospital, but you'll be able to see him every day. I'll take you up there. You can ring him too, but for now, he needs rest and care. So do you."

She shrugged. "I'm fine. It's just a cold."

Her dismissive attitude toward her own health raised his ire. "It's more than that. There's a problem with your transition. You need stabilizing care."

"How do you know so much, Michael? How did you know her?"

He grinned at her waspish tone. "I've known her a long time, I told you that. We went to school together, then medical school. She went off and concentrated on her specialty while I became a surgeon. Since my accident, I've focused on general healthcare, like the clinic work."

Lissa frowned. "But if you're a surgeon, what are you doing working at a free clinic in the middle of Nowheresville?"

His laugh barked loud in the silence. "I couldn't operate immediately after my therapy. Sara suggested I might be able to offer some kind of assistance. I was only going to fill in for a couple of weeks, but you know, there's something about giving back."

"But you came here with us?"

He smiled. "I did. You both needed me more than the clinic. There are other doctors there for the next week or two and I wasn't going to be logged on, so I felt that this was the best use of my time."

"Fine, but since things are going so swimmingly, why haven't you returned to surgery? Why waste your time in general practice?"

That question was direct, and he had to pause and think seriously about it. "I want to, someday. But I'm not ready yet. The strange thing is, I never even really thought about it until you asked." Every word he spoke was true. He wasn't ready to investigate what it was about this woman that made him reconsider everything he knew and held dear.

She wasn't a beauty. Her prickly nature made her difficult to feel close to, and yet, she drew him like no other woman ever had. And this was only after less than two days. Alarm bells jangled in his brain.

"I can't answer all your questions right now, Lissa. All I can say is I felt it was important for me to be there and assist you and Clarrie. Now, let's leave it at that, okay?"

Suddenly, he needed distance between them, and he stood and stepped away from the bed where they'd settled her.

"I'm going to get settled. You've got the remote for the vid screen, lunch will be here shortly, and you should be able to video call with Clarrie later today. I'll be back soon."

She stilled, face pale but exuding a calm visage. "Sure. You go settle in."

For all her words, he knew she'd read his thoughts and was retreating. He sighed, reached out, but she held still.

"Go on. I'll be fine."

When he left her, it was as if he was retreating from her, and his stomach churned as he strode to his door.

He'd chosen his action, now he needed to find a way to mitigate the damage he may have unsuspectingly inflicted with his retreat.

CLARISSA SIGHED and reclined against the pillows. She'd honestly believed she'd never be quite so comfortable again, yet here she was with a soft pillow, heavy warm blankets, and clean clothing she hadn't stolen from someone else. She'd even managed to enjoy a brief sonic shower. Not as good as a water one, but she felt clean again. That rated highly in her books.

Now she was stuck in a hospital, and that brought its own issues. She had no clue how she'd pay for the treatment, even though Michael had claimed he would attend to that. Health care sure didn't come cheap and never was it truly free. Unless he... She ended that thought before it could form fully.

If she'd had thoughts or questions about what Michael would have said, she ignored them. Instead, she tried to scrub any personal feelings from her mind. He was a doctor and only interested in her as a body. That could be the only reason he'd watched her, his eyes roaming over her body. There wasn't any personal interest.

She closed her eyes and forgot about her concerns for now. The fluids they were pumping into her veins, along with the antibiotics, must be quick acting. She sighed, turned, and plumped the pillows. A knock had her opening her eyes and watching the door as it opened slowly.

Sara, the doctor, entered the room. "Good. I see they have you hooked up. I've asked

them to place you on a light diet for now, and we'll take a look tomorrow to see when you can eat fully. Mariah will be in soon with your tray. Do you have any questions?"

Clarissa scanned the woman, surprised that she hadn't tossed her from these hallowed halls. After all, she was a homeless itinerant.

"Alyssa?"

She scowled. "How do I know you can keep me safe like you said? After all, Jer—" Clarissa swallowed the name, but Sara leaned in and frowned.

"Who?"

Clarissa shook her head, but it was too late.

"I heard Jer... So let me think who it could be. I only know of a few other researchers who have experience in this field. The only one I know of with the letter J is Jeremy. Jeremy Colvert, from the Colvert Clinic. But he specializes in prosthetic implementation, and has for years, along with in vitro fertilization. His interest in BioOrganic treatment is years old. And he's not been practicing for... *OhmyGod!* It wasn't him, was it?"

Sara's face took on a look of extreme panic and concern.

"He's been very quiet, and the small amount of research he's published was based on beginning of life and efficacy of..." She looked nauseous, her skin taking on a slightly green tinge.

Terror flooded Clarissa. Sara had worked out who Jeremy was, and if he caught wind of where Clarissa was hiding, there'd be no hole safe enough for her to hide in. Clarissa swung her legs over the side of the bed, even as Sara stepped up to stop her.

"No, you can't leave. We need to find out the truth."

Clarissa didn't want her to find out the totality of how she'd been stripped bare of her humanity. To do so would render her little more than a quivering mass of nothing. She was done with being a victim and a shell.

"Let me out of here." She bit the words out, pushing against Sara who remonstrated with her.

Clarissa tugged at the line snaking into her wrist while Sara hit a tiny button at the side of the bed.

The door slid open, and two burly guards raced in. "You need help, doc?"

"I need her back in the bed, then I need Dr. Michael Villede in the room next door. Get him, quickly."

Clarissa struggled, but the poor condition of her body and lack of nourishment made her easy to overcome. The guard had her hauled back on the bed and was fastening her to the bed before she knew what was happening.

"You gotta stay still, girlie. Don't wanna hurt you. Please." The guard looked at her, his face pleading, and she subsided, realizing that as much as she was hurting him, she was also damaging herself.

The door opened, and Michael surged inside the room. "What the hell is happening here?"

Sara raised two hands, the symbol of peace, and he stopped, but it was clear how unhappy he was, vibrating with anger.

"Thanks, Dave and Sol."

The guards looked at Sara, and at her nod they melted out of the room, leaving Sara, Michael, and Clarissa, still bound to the bed, behind.

"I know who did this. I worked it out when Lissa said—"

"Please don't..." She reached out in entreaty.

Sara continued, "Dr. Jeremy Colvert from the Colvert Clinic."

Michael spun and looked at Clarissa. "Jeremy Colvert? He did this to you?" Clarissa remained still, unwilling to answer.

"He's the only one I know whose name starts with J and has had any interest in BioOrganic Therapy," Sara said firmly. "But if he has—"

"It's in breach of the 'No Harm' oath." Michael headed to Clarissa, reached out and grabbed her hand. "He did the rest too, didn't he?"

Stubbornly silent, Clarissa simply watched him, noted the dark ring that circled his iris, the ruddy glow that settled on his cheeks, and the tick that had begun at his jaw.

Yet even in the face of total fury, his touch remained tender, and that confused her further.

▭

MICHAEL HAD to get a grip on himself. The extremes of his anger both surprised him and yet it wasn't quite unexpected. He took his oaths seriously, and the 'No Harm' that replaced the archaic Hippocratic Oath was one he believed in.

But worse of all was the knowledge that Lissa—and he still wondered what her real name was—had been tortured by someone whom he'd considered an expert in his area of therapy.

"Lissa, he won't get near you. I won't allow it."

"Clarissa." She mumbled the name, and he hovered closer.

"What?"

"My name is Clarissa. Lissa is a name I chose with Clarrie so Jeremy wouldn't find me.

But that's a moot point now, isn't it?" She gave a long sigh and glanced up at him, dusky eyelashes framing her eyes and drawing him in. "It's easy to say he won't find me here, but he's got so many contacts. So many others who work with him. The minute he hears, he'll know, so there's no point hiding who I am now."

"Tell me who and I'll ensure they have no access to you or Clarrie or even your records. I can have them locked down—" Sara's words were cut off by Clarissa.

"Oh, that's fucking rich." Clarissa tugged against the bindings, her face dark and harsh in the artificial light. "You don't have any idea, do you? There were so many that came and went. He not only allowed others access, he watched and egged them on. If they're here, they'll have no concerns at circumventing any restrictions you put in place. To think that you can somehow weed them out is stupidity." Her tone was waspish, and Michael watched her eyes narrowing with spite.

"But Clarissa, we can..."

"Leave it with me, Sara. I'll talk to Clarissa and see if we can't come up with some kind of plan."

Clearly Sara wasn't happy with that. Her lips drooped then firmed before she opened them to frame her argument, but Michael shook his head.

"You've got other patients to see, and I can stay here with Clarissa as long as she needs."

He waited, hoping Sara would take the hint. She did, spinning on her heels, but even as she left the room, she turned her head back to pin him with a furious glare. "Michael, I want to know everything. I can't help if I'm not part of the discussion." Then she went, pulling the door shut after herself.

Michael made his way over to the chair near the bed and sat down heavily. "Jeremy Colvert, eh? Never liked him. He always struck me as an arrogant git, too full of himself and too much money to think he had to abide by any rules."

He glanced at Clarissa, surprised by the glint in her eyes.

"I was going out with him. There was an accident, apparently. I don't know a lot, but he spoke to my parents, I saw him. He said he had tried to save me, but I don't think he did."

She spoke quietly, as if each word stole a portion of her soul. "I was a nanny with a family in the Retrogrand area. He'd been a guest at the house, and we met there. He asked me to the opera and...I liked him."

The words hurt Michael deeply. That Clarissa had been treated so poorly, that he'd shown careless disregard and likely had groomed her was sick and twisted. *Rather like the man himself*, Michael thought.

"So, what happened next?" He reached out, knowing instinctively that she needed his support to get through what would come after that.

"I woke up, fastened to a bed, others coming and going. Then he turned up. I didn't understand at first, but he told me he'd chosen me, that there'd been others, but I was the one he personally wanted. He hurt me."

He squeezed her hand. "How?"

"They experimented. Burns and shocks, cutting and other things." She turned her head away, facing the wall, and he felt a cold weight in the pit of his belly.

"Sexual stuff?"

She clammed up, but he saw the rise and fall of her chest. "He gave them free rein. They didn't touch me like that or even rape me. It was other things. They told me I wasn't human and I had no rights. That I was a thing he'd brought back to experiment on. That's not right. I'm more than that, aren't I? I have rights, don't I?" Now she shifted, her eyes hungry for validation. Her gaze wide and unblinking.

"You do. Just like me, you have to prove yourself as stable, but what you've done with Clarrie, the care you've shown, and the fact that you're willing to work with me—"

"No. I'm not going to tell you more if you intend to use it against him. He'll find me and take me back. Then I'll have nothing. Be nothing. That won't happen, doctor."

He sighed and scrubbed a shaking hand over his aching eyes. She'd started putting up thicker walls, the kind she kept between herself and everyone else. Everyone except Clarrie.

He understood her fears and concerns more than anyone else ever could. "If he isn't called to account for his actions, if we allow him to do this again, others will suffer. You don't want that to happen, do you, Clarissa?"

She closed her eyes and the droop of her mouth pierced him. "Look, I want to be me again. I want to study at University and become a teacher. I want to have friends. I want my life back. They're all things he stole from me."

"Then I'll help you. Jeremy may think he's never going to be caught, and he might think he has resources that set him above everyone else, but I've got contacts too, and we'll use them to make him face the scales of justice. You just have to believe in me and trust me."

The grip of her fingers turned hard, and he stared at her, willing her to open her eyes and look in his direction.

"I don't suppose you'd start by unfastening me then?"

He grinned at her words but leaned over and removed the restraints.

In her smile of thank you, there was more than a glimmer of hope, and it warmed his heart.

Chapter 9

Clarissa had the suspicion she had agreed to something bigger and more encompassing than anything else she'd ever considered. It was scary, but knowing more about Michael, that he was like her and in her corner, gave her a small amount of comfort. Very small. She smiled.

She did want her life back. She didn't want to have to hide who and what she was because of something Jeremy had done to her. How others had used and abused her.

"I want to believe you, doctor."

"Michael."

Clarissa blinked at his dry tone.

"My name is Michael, and I'd like you to use it, especially if I'm going to help you regain your life."

"Okay then, Michael. I'm scared, and I don't think I can fail again or let him take me back. If I do, it might break me into tiny pieces."

Telling him that was like peeling the layers of her defenses away and letting him see the softer underbelly that could be so easily hurt.

"I won't, Clarissa. You and me? We're the same, the two sides of a coin." He moved so that he settled on the side of the bed, which dipped under their combined weights.

"I'm not sure how that could be. You're a man and you've got the kind of resources I could only dream of." She spoke quickly while the wild jump of her pulse did a dance of arousal. It was a spike of adrenaline, and she wasn't quite sure where it had come from.

He had such clear eyes, she noticed. A deep green that married perfectly with his sandy hair. Close up, it looked like a mop of silk, and her fingers itched to curl and rub through the softness. His skin was fine, except where his afternoon growth was covered in stubble.

She wanted to hold her breath, but his scent invaded her nostrils, and when she inhaled, attempting to clear her mind, it hit her gut, spearing down past her belly to the area she'd thought wouldn't ever wake again.

Excitement quivered, but she fisted her hands. He might be the same as her, but she was broken on so many levels she knew she'd just drag him down to her plane of misery if she even *thought* about anything more between them.

"There's more to me than that, Clarissa." He raised a hand, cupped her cheek, and she almost vibrated at his touch. "I'll never hurt you. I give you my word."

Mesmerized, she watched as he came closer, his lips skating over her cheek while her mind and body went into overdrive.

Pull away, her mind screamed while the rest of her body wanted to arch in and accept the tenderness he offered. "I... Uh..."

He pulled back, his gaze scanning over her. "Clarissa, I would like..."

She watched in fascination as he struggled with intense emotions.

"It's okay, Dr. Michael. I get it."

He jerked away as if stung. "Yeah. Look, I promise he won't touch you." The words sounded hollow, and he glanced away.

She reached out, amazed when his nerves jumped as she noted his averted eyes and flattened lips.

"I should go." He made to rise, but she gripped his arm, willing him to stay.

"No. Stay with me. Talk to me. Tell me about who you were before."

With a sigh he settled back to the edge of the bed. "What do you want to know?"

"I'd like to know about Michael, the boy and man. Not so much the doctor," she said, hoping he'd understand the underlying message in her words.

He swung around, their gazes colliding.

"I grew up locally. My mother was a doctor, and my father an inventor of some note. I had a great childhood. My sister and brother were close to me, and when they grew up to be an agent and a senator, it wasn't a surprise. My sister's in a position of authority. She was involved in the re-writing of the old Hippocratic Oath that became the 'No Harm'. I went to medical school—which was where I met Sara—and decided surgery was my thing."

He paused, and Clarissa fluttered her hands, telling him wordlessly to continue.

"She and I were friends through med school, not that we had a lot of time to do anything except exchange textbooks." He smiled, and that tiny change took him from gorgeous to drop- dead sexy, and she sucked in a deep breath while her mind processed the change.

"So why didn't you... You know, after?"

He barked a laugh. "I thought about it in the last couple of months of our internship. Then she was busy initially with her work as a medical researcher and I was enjoying myself. I was a semi-professional athlete. A tennis player."

She sat up. "Really? That's something I wanted to try, but I never had time. Nannies don't get a lot of free time, and I usually used mine doing washing or catching up with my friends."

"Once you're out of here, I'll take you down to the sports center and you can try it out." He spoke with such ease, yet she wouldn't hold Michael to that promise.

"Tell me about growing up." Her demand was met by a small laugh.

"It was a normal childhood. I grew up in the west of town. My parents owned an estate, so we all had plenty of room. With grassed grounds and room for my dog, Chowie. He passed when I was eleven, and it devastated me. That's when my parents urged me to find an activity, and I ended up with tennis. After that, study and tennis kept me busy. For a while I considered going pro. I was achieving scores that would have allowed me to do that. But then I'd look at my mother—she's a cardiologist—and know she was making a real change in people's lives. That's what decided it for me."

Clarissa slumped back in the bed, thinking over his words. "My parents are great too. I hate that they think I'm dead. I went around there once, I told you that, didn't I?" Michael nodded, and she jerked her gaze to the ceiling. "My sister and brother were there too. I miss them. A lot."

"You can have it back, all of it. All you need to do is tell me more about what Jeremy did. How he abused you. I've got contacts. My sister and brother are just the start."

His sister was a senator, his brother an agent. He had money and resources. Could he keep her safe?

"Why would you do this, Michael? I mean, you could turn your back and ignore it all. I could just go away, and you wouldn't need to do anything. So why?" The burning need to know bloomed.

"Because I don't want you to feel such pain. I want to help you. I feel something for you I don't understand, and I want to investigate it. I'm a man who needs to understand what makes things happen."

Clarissa gulped. "You feel something for me?"

"I do."

Michael's soft words restarted the haphazard tattoo of her heartbeat.

"I need time, Michael. I can't just go from nothing to hoping for everything again. It's not that simple for me. And I... Trusting is hard."

"I understand, Clarissa." This time when he rose, she let him go, as the drag of exhaustion pulled at her. "Take a nap, and I'll be back. I'll make sure you've got guards outside the door and only Mariah, from catering, Sara, or myself will be admitted."

She gave a small, tight nod and closed her eyes, her head aching with everything she'd learned.

Chapter 10

Michael left the room. It was understandable that Clarissa was tired. So much had happened, and her body was weakened by the life she'd been living. She also remained fearful that Jeremy would try to regain what he'd lost.

He could take a few steps immediately to get the ball rolling on justice.

Back in his room, he touched his watch, anticipating the shine of the holo-pad. He tapped out the number and waited until his sister's harried face filled the green holo-screen.

"Hey, little brother. Is this urgent, or can I get back to you?"

"Normally I'd say I can call back, but this is something that I think would interest you. Can you talk?"

Her eyes narrowed. "What's up, Michael? You've not got yourself in trouble, have you?"

"No, sis, I haven't. But I've got a friend who needs your assistance. Is there anyone in earshot?"

She rose and disappeared from sight. From the thud that echoed, he knew she'd shut the door to her home office. Then she returned to his view, sitting down heavily.

"So, tell me what you've got."

He proceeded to do so, pleased she allowed him to run through the facts without interruption.

"You're sure it was Jeremy Colvert?"

"Yeah. She knew him beforehand."

Daniella rubbed a finger over her brow. "We need to bring David in on this too. This is huge stuff. You've got her secured?"

He nodded. "I have, but Jonah and Franklin would be welcome." His two buddies from his GMC days had also been his aides and personal guards. Both were brawny, and with their extensive military service, Michael knew if anyone could keep her safe, it was them.

"Give me a few hours to clear my calendar and let me contact David, okay? We'll be there as soon as we can."

The screen blanked, and his fingers itched to click his brother's contact details, but he knew Daniella was right. She usually was.

A tap at the door had him rising. "Who's there?"

"Catering."

He opened the door and frowned as an unfamiliar face filled the opening.

"I've got your lunch."

The trolley was wheeled in, and his muscles tensed. "Where's Mariah?"

"She's off sick."

Tiny alarms went off in his brain. "Thank you. Leave it there and I'll deal with the rest." He waited as the man. disappeared through the closing door, then caught it before it clicked. He peered out into the corridor and watched the man grab another tray, which he deposited in front of the guards.

The guards lifted their cups to their lips and sipped.

The catering officer continued to dither around, as if checking the order. Suddenly, the guards slumped.

Michael hissed and gathered his scattered wits. Whoever the man was, he wasn't from the hospital or catering.

The man pushed a cart to Clarissa's door, sat the two guards up in their seats, pulling their caps down over their eyes as if they were resting, then shoved open her door.

Michael waited until he was inside before pulling his own door fully open. Then he charged, moving on swift feet and shoving the wooden barrier out of the way.

Once inside he stilled, as the man held a tiny laser pistol on Clarissa.

"You shouldn't have followed me."

The man aimed the gun at Michael, who pivoted, pleased to have his bio-cybenetic strength and speed.

The burst of light grazed his flesh, but he bared his teeth and sprang. Michael landed on the man with an *oomph* and an almost inaudible crunch. The sudden jerking action of the man beneath him was reminiscent of the war, and for a moment, he was flung back into his memories of death and destruction. The man slumped and stilled on the floor.

The tang of bitter almonds whispered in the air. "Cyanide," he said softly. Clarissa blinked, and Michael sighed. "He's dead."

Michael pushed himself off the body, angry with himself and the dead man on the floor. "Are you..." Clarissa's voice wobbled a little. "...all right?"

He glanced at her. She was as white as a sheet while her gaze settled on him, and fear gnawed at his guts.

"I'm fine. He didn't manage to hurt you, did he? Didn't inject you or..."

She shook her head. "I'm not the one with a laser strike. Now come here and let me see how bad it is." She flung off the sheet and twisted, and he noted the way her hospital gown gaped at the back. He hadn't noticed that before, nor the fine shaking of her lips and hands.

"I'll be fine." He didn't think he could handle her being near him, almost naked, while the surge of his emotions continued to overwhelm him.

"Don't be a baby. Sit down and let me grab a clean, damp cloth."

She climbed down from the bed, reaching for the basin and a cloth that hung from a hook. When she turned he caught sight of her back and further down, her rounded buttocks. Blood rushed to his face, and elsewhere too, so he had to close his eyes, count to ten, and yet it wasn't enough.

"Michael?" She'd returned and he hadn't heard her. She touched him and he groaned. "You're badly hurt, aren't you?"

Anguish filled her voice, and he reached out, blindly groping for her hand. When he trapped it, her pulse fluttered like the beat of a butterfly's wings. He dragged her closer, opened his eyes, and surveyed her face. "I'm going to kiss you."

Then he did.

CLARISSA FELT THE TOUCH, the way his lips settled over hers while the buzz of reaction continued. It had felt like the crawl of dozens of ants in her belly until he kissed her. Now there were a million sensations as hunger and need warred with pleasure.

Too much! Her brain tried to decipher it all. Images and flashes appeared on her eye screen, and she blinked, clearing her vision so all she saw was him.

The overload of sensations had her eyes closing, simply accepting the gentle action for a moment.

He pulled away. "Please get in the bed." He breathed heavily, his chest moving roughly, and she frowned.

"Why?"

"Because if you don't, I'm going to strip that ugly gown off you and do something neither of us is ready for."

She gaped. "I..."

"Please."

Without a word she watched as he turned away, and she climbed in, settling the gown over her body then the sheets. "I'm in."

He turned, and the ruddy glow of his face amazed her.

"Press the alert buzzer while I check the guards outside."

She did so quietly, surprised at how calm he suddenly sounded while her brain was still trying to process the kiss and the effects of his touch and words on her body and brain.

Lying there, she inspected the ceiling and waited for him to return. When he did, his face was grim. "The guards will live, but you can't stay here. I'm going to arrange for Sara to release you to my care. Then I'm taking you home with me. The hospital here might have adequate security, but nothing will get inside my compound."

His eyes glinted with a light from deep within, and she knew what that meant—he'd activated every one of his cybernetic senses. For a second, she wondered if it was to deal with the issue of the dead assassin and damaged guards, or the passionate encounter they'd shared.

Michael shuffled over to the wardrobe and sighed before pulling out a robe. He flung it toward her. "Put this on and we'll get out of here. Go to my room."

She bit her lip. "What about Clarrie?"

Michael sighed heavily. "I don't have the facilities in my home, so he's going to have to stay here. But I can get him moved to the ICU, that will mean he's under constant watch. I'll scare up some guards for him too."

It didn't feel like nearly enough, but she nodded. "Okay then."

He turned away as she crawled halfway down the bed, thus avoiding touching the now- dead assassin.

Once she had pulled on the wrap, he grabbed her close and hurried her out of the room.

Chapter 11

Michael waited as his sister entered his home office. "Indications are the man had a cyanide dental implant. You're right about the danger Clarissa's in. All we could find on his communicator was a directive to get her and neutralize the threat."

"Who sent the threat, and where did it come from?"

Daniella shrugged, her golden hair bobbing as she settled into the easy chair in front of his desk. "We don't know. It's to a burner account and that's since been erased. What little my people could find out was scrambled. I've asked David to bring in some agents. He might be able to suss out more."

Michael sighed and rubbed his aching forehead.

"Mike, I have to ask why is she so important to you that you'd get in the middle of this? You're already a target with the authorities since your treatment."

He knew exactly what she meant. "She's like me, Dani, except she was treated without permission. I don't think it was even the result of an accident, although she's adamant that was the only reason he chose her. I think she was groomed. He'd been sniffing around and—"

"And you're emotionally involved, aren't you? Have you slept with her?"

He tensed, fury coursing. "What business is that of yours?"

Daniella leaned closer to him. "It's a question you're going to have to field. By asking it now, I'm preparing you. You can't go off and get angry. That will only fuel the situation further, brother."

"To answer the question, no. Not that I don't want to, but she's raw and hurting. I don't take advantage of women who need my help. While I may have hopes, I also have no intention of hurrying her or pressing any kind of advantage."

Daniella steepled her fingers. "Mother and Father will like her. She's soft even with the experiences she's had. There's something nurturing about—"

"I think it's in her DNA. She was a nanny. And she'd make a great mother."

"Whoa there! Just how involved are you?"

"All the way." It didn't hurt to say the words; instead, he grinned and felt lighter than he had in a long time. Indeed, he was sure she was the only one for him. "Okay then, so the sooner Mother and Father meet her, the better."

He frowned at his sister's words. "Why?"

"Because that takes the pressure off David and me. I don't plan on having kids until I meet the right man, and David needs time to court the woman he's got his eyes on. You keep our parents busy and we've got time to do our own thing!"

Michael detected a hint of urgency in her tone. "They've been giving you a hard time?"

"Mother asked how long she'd have to wait for the clock to start ticking, so yes, you could say it's getting difficult."

He stood and roamed to his desk, placing a hand on the coffee machine. "Want one?"

"Of course I do."

He poured two coffees while he thought over her words. Children. Until now, he'd never considered that, but the problem was, he wasn't sure if they could, given the nano-tech that roamed through their bodies, or even if Clarissa felt the same. Discussing it with his sister seemed forward, and yet...

But from Clarissa's physical state and her refusal to answer some questions, he thought perhaps she knew more about that. The sour taste that resided in his mouth whenever he considered how she'd been tortured increased.

"By the way, make sure you get her to wear this." Daniella slung something silvery at him, and without a conscious thought, he caught the tiny bracelet and held it up to the light.

"What is it?"

"A tracker. That way if they do get hold of her again, we can find her."

Michael frowned. He wasn't keen on the tagging that he'd had to undergo, but at least this gave him time to broach that with her. He shoved the trinket into his pocket. "I'll do it later today."

A rap on the door captured his attention.

"Come in," he called out.

It opened, and Clarissa entered, now dressed in a loose pair of pants and a jumper that matched the blue of her eyes. His breath caught in his throat.

"Oh, I didn't realize you had company." She started to back out, but Michael gestured for her to join them.

"This is my sister, Daniella. She's outspoken but damned good at her stuff. Don't let her power suit put you off."

Clarissa smiled and his stomach lurched.

"Coffee?" he asked.

"Yes, please."

He grabbed a third cup and placed it on the tray after he'd filled it with the dark brew.

Then he took a jug of cream from the small fridge and lastly checked to make sure sugar and sugar replacements were there along with some teaspoons.

He carried the tray over and placed it on the small coffee table and settled into a chair. "Grab a seat, and we can talk about what we know."

Clarissa lowered herself into the closest chair to him, and he couldn't help reaching out and grasping her hand.

"That suits you. I'm glad I was right about the color." he said.

She blushed a little, and satisfaction flowed through him.

"Uh, yeah." She tugged her hand away, reached forward, and grasped a coffee mug before adding cream.

Daniella watched them for a moment, a gleam of deep emotion in her eyes.

"So, Clarissa. Michael gave me your full name, and I've run your history. According to the reports we found, it seems you were involved in an accident while on your way to the opera with Jeremy Colvert, who you've stated was the person who undertook the therapy without your agreement. Is that correct?"

Clarissa sat bolt upright in the chair, her face devoid of emotion. "Yes."

"All right then. I can find a listing of an accident, but on the same day three other women disappeared. I've got my personal assistant doing some digging, but they were all about the same size as you. It's believed they all had a suitor who picked them up and took them to places including the zoo, the movies, and on occasion, to the museum. Is that the same as your experience?"

Clarissa stiffened. "He was doing it to other women?"

Daniella pursed her lips. "I'm thinking he was grooming women, while preparing for the bio-cybernetic implants at the same time. He doesn't have access to priority production lines that Sara had for Michael. So, he's likely creating his own chipsets and implants. Which means he's knowingly working outside the 'No Harm' standards all medical personnel must agree to before registration. My personal research has also concluded that since his accident he's been seen in public places with a range of women. Interestingly enough, many of them have met an unprepossessing end. Car accidents, boating accidents, and the like. Mostly in situations that have raised no alarms, and his companions are either poorly connected or have no families. That in and of itself is unusual and raises questions for me."

Clarissa bit her lip and looked away. "He's a monster."

"He is. But the best thing is, with your help, we can stop him, so he won't be able to do something like this ever again. He'll never take a woman and make her suffer the way he's done with you."

Michael watched as Clarissa took a sip of her coffee, closed her eyes, and held still. "Getting him won't be enough though. He had others who were experimenting."

Clarissa opened her eyes, and her gaze settled on Daniella.

Daniella nodded. "Yes. David, our brother, will be here soon. He's managed to obtain a Presidential Warrant and we've got an idea where his lab was situated. David's got agents who will storm the building, and they'll find whatever records there are. I don't think we'll get Jeremy at the same time, but once we begin the process, his days are numbered. They'll get records and collect evidence that will help us put him away for a long, long time."

With a clatter, Clarissa placed her coffee cup down on the table. "Would you excuse me? I'm suddenly feeling a little off."

She rose and left the room. Michael started to follow her, but Daniella grabbed his hand. "Let her go. The reality is huge, and she has to understand that this is the only way."

"She's hurting, Daniella, and my job is to heal." He pulled away and hurried after Clarissa.

THAT JEREMY WOULD BE CALLED to account was scary, and yet it filled Clarissa with hope.

That wasn't what upset her, as much as knowing there were others. Not just one or two. Clarissa had vacillated and refused to offer assistance. She'd run while potentially other women faced the same horror she had.

She'd allowed her weakness to blind her to a reality that sickened her to the depth of her being. Clarissa wrapped shaking arms around herself, wondering if she'd ever be safe again.

The door opened behind her and Michael strode in.

"I was weak, Michael. He's probably got another woman, or women, and is doing the same to them while I ran and hid." She pushed her nails into the flesh of her arms, hoping for the sting to wake her up from this bad dream. It didn't, so Clarissa refused to look at him while shame burgeoned.

"No, Clarissa. You can't take on the responsibility for others you knew nothing about. He would have done so whether you were there or not. Besides, Daniella checked and he's only just started the pattern again in the last few days. He was seen with a girl at the museum and another at a play. He's clever enough to realize that he needs to keep a low profile between attempts."

"Then why haven't the authorities tried before?" Tears trickled down her cheeks and she swiped at them, but he stilled her hands, rubbing soft thumbs over the tear tracks.

"Don't cry. Without you, we wouldn't be as far along, and no one would know what he was doing. You alone, standing up, has made the capture of this monster a reality."

She bit her lip while his tender touches left her senses swimming.

"But I should have done more."

He didn't argue with her, just pulled her gently forward so his lips touched hers. She opened to him, while he drew her in, swamping her senses so there was only the two of them and the ache that grew down low in her belly.

His hands slid from her face, over her shoulders, and around her waist. Their bodies touched, hip-to-hip and breast-to-chest.

She was a mass of quivering sensations, her nipples tightening to nubs as they dragged against him, even through the layers of clothing.

The kiss changed, deepened until he ravished her, lips and tongue working, hands kneading her butt, and she curled her hands in his hair.

It lasted forever but was over too soon. When he pulled away, she heaved, trying to suck in oxygen to fill her empty lungs.

"Michael..."

"This isn't a one-off attraction, you understand that, don't you?"

She nodded, well aware that what she wanted was more than the simple act of sexual intercourse. The hunger that had kept gnawing at her belly grew with each touch.

But she wasn't ready yet. Too many things had happened. Too much loss and pain had been heaped upon her. She needed time to understand and trust him fully with that. "You don't have the stuff in your head that I've got."

He sighed and laid his forehead against hers. "Whatever baggage you come with, I'm up for. I want to be with you. Only you. I don't care what it takes, so long as you want to be with me too."

Tears pricked again. No matter what he thought he knew, he didn't have the experience of the nightmares, the pain.

She tugged away, but he held on. "Michael, you don't understand. I'm broken and not sure I can ever again feel safe. I have nightmares and—"

He cut off her words, his soft finger sliding along the seam of her lips. "We'll work through it together. That's what partnerships are about."

Clarissa wanted so badly to believe him, but he wanted more than she was sure she could give. She sighed. "Let's take it one day at a time. That way if you feel you can't cope with my problems, there's no harm, no foul."

His lips firmed, a flash of fire in his gaze, and she refused to see what her vision screen described as dissatisfaction and anger.

———

THE TINY, hand-held communicator in Michael's pocket blared, and he dug it out and checked the screen, while he kept his other hand firmly twined around Clarissa's.

"David's here. We need to go down and meet with him and Daniella in my office."

He felt the tiny jerk of her hand, as if she tried to disengage herself from him before she spoke. "Okay."

He placed a small kiss on the knuckles where their fingers intertwined.

"What was that for?"

He grinned at the surprise in her voice. "To keep you there."

With those words he led her out of the room and down the staircase toward his office. "You know, I'm not sure I want to keep this house."

She glanced around her. "But why? It's beautiful and old."

"You like it?"

"It's lovely, and I'm sure it reminds you of where you grew up."

He barked with laughter as she spoke, each word carefully considered. "Not really. My parents were into white walls and extensive artwork. I bought this when I finished medical school, but suddenly the dark walls and antiques don't strike me as very family friendly."

She stopped. "Family friendly?" Her words were stilted as if something stuck in her throat.

"Sure. We could take a look at the properties closer to your parents. There'd be a few I think might be of interest."

He waited for her to answer.

"I'm not ready for any of this." Her mutter made him smile until he reached the door of the room where he'd met with Daniella earlier. What lay ahead would tax Clarissa, and he wasn't sure how else to allay her fears.

In silence he grasped the doorknob and pushed it wide. She entered the room, and he sucked in a deep breath then followed her.

Clarissa sat down in the seat she'd vacated earlier. Daniella eyed him as he entered, and he gave a tight smile before giving his brother David a quick, manly hug and slap on the back. "Glad you're here, David."

They settled into seats, and Daniella introduced David to Clarissa. His brother gave him a swift 'this is your girl?' look, and Michael grinned at him.

"So, what have you learned?" Daniella reclined back in her chair, pinning David with a direct gaze.

"As you know, I got the warrant, and the agents are heading for the location right now. They'll enter and execute their search-and-seize warrant, as well as taking those on the ground into custody." David glanced down at his small palm unit, nodding tensely. "The person who broke into Clarissa's room has been identified, however it would seem he was an ancillary staff member ."

Michael stilled. "Clarissa said there'd be contacts at the hospital." He turned to her. "You were right."

She screwed up her face at his words.

David harrumphed, and they returned their attention to him. "He worked in a custodial role and had clearance to access all sections. Security is currently investigating how no one questioned him being in catering at that time and how the two guards weren't tipped off."

Michael frowned. "So, Colvert's likely got at least one person, and maybe more, at the hospital? They've probably been on the lookout for her since she escaped. Status on Clarrie?"

David smiled. "My men describe him as in it for your girl here. He's been demanding updates every five minutes and wants to know when he can connect via link. I've told my men I'll arrange it later today. Apparently, he threw a hell of a tantrum until a time was settled on."

Clarissa grinned. "He's a good man and just worried about me." She leaned in. "He won't get in trouble, will he?"

David reached out and patted her hand. "No. We don't take action for people who are worried about their friends. Actually, he was a veteran of the later African wars of early 2097. He's entitled to a lot of support and that will see him right. He didn't know, which is why he was living on the street. Once my men explained it to him, he was thankful you were there for him, so he'd get the chance. He's got a family, and we're going to try and hook him back up with them."

Clarissa sighed. "Then I did a good thing there."

"You've done far better than you ever realized, Clarissa." Michael smiled at her, then reached out to touch her cheek.

David's communicator squarked, and he glanced down at it. "All right, you two lovebirds. If you've finished the touchy-feely part of the session, I have an update."

Michael scowled at his brother. "So?"

"They're in and found several women. One of them in the bio-tank after what is being described as bone regeneration and grafting. Michael, is that what I think it is?" David shoved an image on his communicator under his nose.

Michael's stomach lurched. "Yeah. They've coated the bones in the nano-infused metal coating. They suspend you in a fluid bath until the body has accepted the graft enough to move them."

Daniella sighed. "Now at least we can prove he's undertaking unlawful therapy in an unregistered medical facility."

"Yeah. But it's worse than that. According to my men, they've found records showing at least ten other women have been treated in the facility. Including your records, Clarissa."

She paled. "What else?"

"The men state there is extensive information concerning your torture. They're pulling the records in to be used against him and his team. It also names others involved." David glanced at his brother.

Daniella interrupted, "It's going to be messy, Michael, but what it will do is give me what I need to work on that bill. With this, I can prove that those of you who've been given the technology-based therapy, and especially those who had no choice, should have equal rights under law."

"What does that mean?" Clarissa's question had Michael turning in his seat.

"We have to meet certain standards of behavior, and our movements are tracked so they know where we are in order to ensure we don't participate in any actions that might be dangerous to humanity."

"Which is a crock of—" Daniella surged up, but Michael raised a hand.

"You know that, and I know that, but people get scared about things they don't understand. David has been working day and night to gather the information so I can formulate the arguments. Clarissa's actions will reinforce that there is no change to our thought processes or feelings. We just needed to prove it." He smiled ruefully at Clarissa who frowned.

"Is that why you wanted me to stay? So you could prove—"

"No, Clarissa. Everything I've told you is the truth. I care about you, and I want you in my life."

Now he wondered what he'd done to reinstate the frown lines on her face.

"Clarissa, Michael has never asked a woman to stay with him. He rattles around in this huge house by himself. Don't think because he says you've helped with the cause that it's the reason he wants you around."

———

DEEP DOWN, Clarissa wondered if Michael wanted her or the assistance she could give

him. Which of those was in the ascendancy? She wanted to believe that it was about her, wanted it so intensely her whole body vibrated with it. Of course, so much was going on that she couldn't be sure what was real and what remained a figment of her imagination.

David had said his men were now locking down the clinic, Daniella was arguing that she should believe Michael's words, and he was giving her the I-want-you-to-believe-me look.

"All right, let's focus on Jeremy. Have your men caught him yet?" Michael demanded.

David shook his head. "He's not there, but we didn't expect him to be. If the woman is in the bio-tube, from what the on-scene surgeons have said, he'd be offsite and monitoring her stats remotely."

"What will happen to her?"

"For the moment nothing, Clarissa. If we move her, she'll likely perish, and that's not our aim. So, we'll keep our people there, onsite, where she can be monitored. Sara Windhower will be co-opted to oversee her treatment and to balance anything that needs assistance."

"Okay, so what about me?"

"What about you?"

She leaned forward. "Michael said he had to pass tests. Be checked out. When does that happen for me?"

Daniella cleared her throat. "I've already started the process of petitioning for onsite therapy here. I've spoken to a judge I know, who's had some experience dealing with these kinds of petitions." She looked to Michael who gave a nod. "He's indicated that he'll consider Dr. Aros visiting you here, especially given the current circumstances."

"Dr. Aros?"

Michael groaned. "He was my therapist and the one who signed off on my clearance. I had to do my time in seclusion and under scrutiny at the halfway house and hospital. At least you'll be more comfortable here, won't you?"

His glance was unsure, and while a devil might have raised its head and she nearly said 'no', it occurred to her that it was mean and below her. "I'm happy to stay here, with you, Michael."

"Good. Then I'll progress the petition, and David can continue to direct the search for Jeremy. Michael has the place on lockdown, and your friend...umm..."

"Clarrie," Michael added.

"Oh yes. Clarrie is safe where he is."

"All right, so what do I do in the short term?" Clarissa wondered how she'd fill her time.

On the streets, she'd hunted for food, clothing, and the necessities of life, but here she didn't have a role or any particular thing to do.

"Well, you could enroll in those studies you talked about."

Michael's suggestion surprised her, and she whipped her head around to gaze at him. "But I can't pay the tuition." It was just one more reminder of what had been stripped

from her.

"Under our witness protection scheme, you wouldn't have to pay a cent. We just need to

get your status as deceased overturned, then we can get you set up," Daniella said. She made it sound so easy.

Once again, Clarissa felt amazement at how everything was

falling into place. She wasn't certain it could possibly be as simple as they made out, but hell, anything was better than the limbo she'd existed in for so long.

"So..."

"Leave that with me," David said as he stood up. "Now, I don't know about you lot, but I've got other things to be doing."

Chapter 12

Michael prowled his room. He didn't really see the dark drapes or the comfortable bed. He'd tried several times to contact Franklin and Jonah, but all he got was their answering service. It was eight in the morning, and they should be answering.

The screaming ring of his personal cell had him jumping, then rushing to the small table in front of the bed. He scooped it up. "Michael here."

"Hey, what's with the millions of messages, doc?"

Franklin. Michael closed his eyes and inhaled deeply. "Are you and Jonah on active service currently? I have a personal situation and could really do with your assistance." The words tumbled and fell as he flopped into the armchair beside the table.

"What kind of situation? And yeah, you need us, we'll be there. Jonah is due here in the next couple of minutes... Hang on, I think that's him at the door." Sounds filtered through the earpiece, the thud of a door closing and voices. "Okay, I'm going to put you on speaker."

Another silence, then a crackle. "Hey, doc. Frank says you need our help. What's up?" Jonah always took the lead between the two of them, Franklin bowing to his skill at strategy and organization.

"It's delicate. Can you get over here as soon as possible? I need some assistance with bodyguard duty." He wanted to share more with them, but the situation was far too precarious at the moment. Jeremy was out there somewhere and had assistance from an unknown number of others.

David had left, and though he'd left a couple of his best men on duty, Michael didn't know them, so he couldn't be sure himself of their reliability. Daniella had taken her personal guard with her. And although Michael and Clarissa were there in his personal fortress, he wasn't sure it would be enough to keep her safe. And that wasn't acceptable.

"I can't tell you much more over the phone. I need a face-to-face. How soon?"

"We can be there in about an hour. Should we pack?" Jonah was probably already making notes in his tiny PDA.

"Yeah. This might take a while."

THROUGH THE DOOR of the room Michael had allocated to her, Clarissa heard the knocking.

"Come in."

There wasn't so much as a squeak as the wood parted to admit Sara. "Time for your medicine, Clarissa. Then I have the results of your blood tests and the scans we performed." Sara carried a kidney-shaped dish, which she slid onto a small table. "Sit down and we'll get this out of the way."

Sara tugged on a pair of examination gloves as Clarissa settled into the easy chair and extended her arm.

Sara lifted the syringe, tapped it with her finger, then carefully slid it into Clarissa's flesh. Once she'd disposed of the used implement, she passed over a paper cup and Clarissa downed the tiny purple pill.

"Good. Now, your results show anemia, a hint of giardiasis, and a few other things." Clarissa's heart rate revved, and she made to stand, but Sara lifted a hand, staying her. "Nothing too problematic.

That's a broad-spectrum antibiotic I've prescribed. A couple of days on that should help to clear most things up. But what I do want to talk to you about is a little more...concerning." Sara whipped out a small, hand-held device that clearly had the details of Clarissa's tests. "You have shown signs of more than one pregnancy, but since you didn't disclose it..."

The pit of Clarissa's stomach yawed. How could she tell Sara that they'd done things to her body in order to find out if their *improvements* negated her ability to conceive and carry a child?

"I don't..." Clarissa shook her head, trying hard to blank those memories out.

"There's some scarring, Clarissa. We can repair most of it, but there could be ramifications."

Bile rose, scouring her esophagus. She didn't want to revisit those memories. Along with just about everything else, it tore at her soul. "Please, I really don't want to discuss this." Her voice sounded hoarse, and she pushed up now, ungainly in her need to escape. "Please go."

Clarissa turned away, but she knew Sara hovered. She felt Sara's presence at her back.

"I'll go for now, but we need to discuss this," Sara said. "You may also require the services of—"

"Please! Stop talking about this. Go!" Clarissa wrapped her arms around her middle, gripping the flesh of her arms even as she shouted. She needed to be alone, to find her balance once more. Couldn't Sara see that?

Clarissa heard the door opening and footsteps coming closer. She hunched inward, not expecting a blow, but unwilling to see who was there to view her pain.

"Sara? What are you doing to her?" Michael had made his way into the room.

"See this? I was trying to discuss it with Clarissa and—"

Clarissa heard his inhalation, and she shuddered, knowing Sara had just shown him the one thing Clarissa hadn't fully disclosed because she wasn't ready.

"Get out, Sara." The trembling of his tones meant he too now struggled to accept the truth. Sara had stripped Clarissa of the one secret she'd buried deep in her psyche. Revealed it in its ugly glory, which made her even less human than before.

"I'll be back. Clarissa needs counseling and—"

"Go." He didn't bellow but the intent was there. If Sara didn't leave, he'd forcibly eject her.

He slid his arms around Clarissa, enfolded her like a child, and just held her. Letting her know without words that he understood.

***

"I'M SO SORRY, CLARISSA." Michael was genuinely devastated by the result Sara had thrust upon him. If that was his reaction, he couldn't even begin to understand how Clarissa would feel. "You don't have to stay, Michael. I know you have things to do."

"I have many things I should be doing, that's true," he said. She stiffened in his arms, and he almost smiled. Instead, he propped his chin on the top of her head and whispered, "But most of all, I have your needs. Don't push me away. I need to be here for you. To support you in anything you need or want."

She sagged, accepting his embrace. The one small action speaking volumes.

He waited, quiet and patient, until she stirred and tugged away.

"My friends made contact. They should be here soon. Come down with me and meet them. Franklin and Jonah served with me in the GMC during the war of '42."

Now her lovely brow creased. "GMC?"

"General Medical Corps. Rear-Guard position offering medical support to the front line."

"Oh." Her eyes widened. "But that's not how..."

"No. Car accident. I'll tell you about it later, if that would help?"

Clarissa nodded distractedly. "Your friends? They're doctors too?"

"No. They were my personal guards and aides. We became good friends, and they're both still career military, but in a specialist area. I'm going to co-opt them into your security task force until we get our hands on Jeremy."

"But I don't..."

He stepped forward and grabbed Clarissa's hand, tugging her closer. "You need to be safe. I need to know that you've got the best and someone I trust. Franklin and Jonah are like bears with cubs. No one and nothing will get near you. Now, come downstairs and meet them."

She sighed and looked up at him. He couldn't ignore the primal thrum that pushed him to kiss her. Her lips, soft and tender, parted under his ministrations, and he deepened the connection, clutching her close so their bodies crowded together. His tongue slid within the cavern of her mouth, and she moaned, her hands clutching his shoulders, and his fingers found and caressed her buttocks.

The twin nubs of her breasts grazed his chest, even through layers of clothing. *I need to feel her.* "Clarissa." The word was a query.

Her moan was an answer, and he burrowed his hands under the waist of her jumper. sliding up the flesh he found until his hands settled over her breasts, which were only hidden by the light bra she wore.

Her nipples jutted, and he slid shaking fingers over them as she gyrated against him. His mouth tore away from hers and found the sensitive flesh of her neck.

"Michael," she breathed, and his body, which was already hard, took on the feel of titanium, his cock straining for her.

"I want you so much, Clarissa."

"Please," she mewled, "don't stop."

A fine madness settled in his mind, demanding more.

It was the rapping of knuckles on the door that intruded. "Shit!" He pulled away. Clarissa hurriedly rearranged her clothing as he watched.

"Who..." He had to clear his throat and mind. "Who is it?"

"Mr. Michael, Franklin Mann and Jonah McDowal are here to see you. Shall I admit them?" His housekeeper's voice echoed.

Michael screwed up his face, for a moment cursing the timing of their arrival. Yet he couldn't and wouldn't take advantage he'd told her. Instead, he pulled her along by the hand. "Coming now, Mrs. Hudson."

Chapter 13

The two men waiting in Michael's office were brawny with large, meaty arms and military correct posture. Clarissa stopped, unsure, but the look in their eyes didn't imply pity so much as a guarded interest.

"Thanks for coming, Frank, Jonah. This is Clarissa. She's had a rough time of it as late. But I'll fill you in over breakfast. I'm assuming you're both hungry."

"Could eat a pig right now," the largest man, with a hard-chiseled jaw and bright blue eyes, stated.

The other, dark-haired and brown-eyed, laughed. "You can always count on Frankie to be hungry."

The three men chuckled as if it were an old and well-worn joke.

"Then come through to the dining room. Mrs. Hudson will have some of her special breakfast goodies ready to go."

Michael led them through into a cool tiled room, decorated in muted tones. He pulled out a chair for Clarissa and waited until she was seated before settling himself into the seat beside her. Even as they relaxed, Mrs. Hudson bustled in, carrying a tray of coffee.

"It's good to see you boys again. Michael and Clarissa are just about to eat, and I take it you boys would like some bacon? Eggs? What about mushrooms?"

"Mrs. H, if I could afford you, I'd whisk you off and marry you so I could enjoy your home cooking every day," Frankie teased the older woman, and she bussed his arm.

"None of that, my boy. Now let me go and I'll get some food on." She scurried away. "Clarissa, are you okay to tell them your part, or do you want me to explain?"

It was as if he understood her need to be somewhat in charge of her life, and she couldn't help the tiny squeeze of her heart. "Would you?"

The telling was painful, but for the first time, she had someone who understood and treated her as an equal. Someone who knew the pain and suffering she'd experienced, even if he could never fully appreciate the loss of trust or terror of those experiments.

With few words, Michael explained about the circumstances, how she'd been manipulated and tortured. The two men listened, their gazes sharpening. Partway through his recitation, Frankie pulled an old-fashioned notebook from his pants pocket and started making notes, but they remained silent until Michael had told them everything.

"You expect him to try to retrieve Clarissa?" Jonah took a sip of his coffee and gazed into the cup as if it were a guidebook.

"I do. He tried at the hospital, but we were able to overpower the man. I think it was more of an impromptu attack rather than considered. Colvert's always been very methodical in his actions. At least until now."

"Right then. We'll need a look at your security systems. You'll both be on lockdown. I'll need the names and IDs of those who'll be granted access. Everything in and out will be inspected. Until this man is apprehended, you're in danger, Clarissa. We won't let him near you though. We'll die before that happens."

She bit her lip. "I... Thank you. I really don't know what else to say." Flustered and at sea, she simply shook her head.

Michael grasped her hand. "I appreciate this. A lot, guys."

At that moment, Mrs. Hudson entered the room, carrying a tray piled high with food, including slabs of sizzling bacon, a dish of eggs, and another with mushrooms. "Don't know about you, but planning makes me hungry, and you boys always have an appetite." She slid the platters onto the table in front of them and retreated with a grin.

Chapter 14

Clarissa listened to the men's banter while picking at her food, wondering if she'd ever feel so free again.

"We could set up a sting operation." Jonah picked up his coffee cup and drank deeply.

Michael vehemently shook his head. "No. Clarissa has been through enough already. I won't risk her to that butcher. If it went wrong..."

The food in her belly congealed, but she understood what Jonah was getting at. It would bring the situation to an end. She'd be free to go, and that meant—

The thought stopped there. Where would she go? To her parents? She didn't know if she was ready for that just yet. She was nowhere near the girl they remembered. She'd changed, and not just physically.

"It would jeopardize the planning that Daniella and David are doing, wouldn't it?" she asked.

Michael pinned her with his gaze. "Probably, but besides that, I wouldn't let you do it anyway."

She held up her hand. "I didn't mean that I was comfortable, or even planning on going ahead with the idea, but merely clarifying the situation in my mind."

When Michael grimaced, she placed her hand over his. "I'm sorry. This is all so new. You don't know me well enough to understand how I think. I like to know what's happening. I have a need to understand things. I've always been like that. At least until recently."

His thumb rubbed back and forth over her hand as she spoke.

"I agree, using Clarissa as bait isn't appropriate, but we could use a bait. Someone he'd never expect." Franklin leaned toward the table. "What if a medical researcher wanted more? Needed that edge? Your friend Sara would do it, I'm sure. When I met her after your accident, she was driven, looking for ways to extend the benefits of her therapeutic use of this technology. It wouldn't really be that great a leap."

Michael shook his head again. "He'd smell a rat. Clarissa is here in my care—"

"A fact that has been kept under wraps. As far as anyone except your brother's operatives, the ICU staff with her friend Clarrie, and us, no one else is aware she's left the hospital. You've got the room sealed as if she were still there. Guards outside it twenty-four- seven. We could make it work. It's not inconceivable."

"And she could get inside and..." Michael's words trailed off as his face turned ruddy and his hand tensed on the cutlery, his knuckles turning white.

Clarissa withdrew her hand. He might say he wasn't involved with Sara, but here he was showing otherwise. She'd be best to distance herself now. Before she came unstuck. The jangle of the bracelet he'd given her last night tinkled, and he glanced in her direction as she reached for the napkin in her lap. Clarissa twisted it, wondering how soon she could leave the planning session around the dining table.

"No. Sara is not some kind of lure you can throw out there. She's a human..."

At that point it became too much. Clarissa murmured her excuses and fled the room, heading for the outside. She'd discovered the small rose garden at the side of the house and hurried there, seeking solitude as she worked through what they'd discussed around the table.

Hearing the discussion reinforced to Clarissa how different she now was. Not in terms of strength or even character, but how she'd be in danger of becoming a commodity. A blunt instrument in the waging of war and power, without feelings or a soul. The thought depressed her.

A sound captured her attention, and she began turning as a pad slid over her mouth.

The cloying sweetness enveloped her senses. She reached but the darkness crashed down on her...

MICHAEL LEFT THE TABLE, aware that Clarissa had been concerned by something that had been said, given that she'd become silent. Then she'd left the room. He'd given her a minute, sure she'd be waiting outside the room, just beyond the doors.

But she wasn't, and disquiet washed over him. Jonah and Franklin joined him.

"Where did she go?" He couldn't contain the puzzlement, and the growing sense of concern that spread like tendrils through his gut. "Jonah, go upstairs and check the room closest to mine. See if she's there."

His brain whispered that he was blowing his worry out of proportion, but his instincts were screaming at him to hurry and find her.

Jonah zipped around Michael, his gait sure and speedy, while Franklin moved to the downstairs rooms, opening doors methodically.

When the front door opened wide, Michael released the pent-up breath, sure she'd enter the foyer. Instead, it was one of David's men. "Uh, the lady went to the garden around the side. I hung back but heard a noise. When I went to investigate, I couldn't find her. I've already alerted the other guards, and they're beginning a full search."

The man looked dazed, and Michael peered at him. "What happened to you?" A closer look showed glassy eyes and a tiny ribbon of drool curling down one side of his chin. "Sit down." He steered the guard to the bottom step.

"I don't know. I just felt odd after I'd looked for the girl, Clarissa. It was sudden...." Then the man slumped to the side, eyes closed and breathing shallow.

"There has to be a dart or something, Frank. Help me find it." Michael started tugging at the man's clothes, checking around collars when his fingers felt a small, plastic item. "Here."

He held up the tiny dart-ended pellet.

"Dammit. They've probably got Clarissa too." Michael's heartbeat sped up as adrenaline surged. He tossed his communicator to Franklin. "Get hold of my sister, Daniella. Tell her what's happened and get her men onto tracking where Clarissa's been taken. Jonah, help me get this guard into the sitting room. I can do a test and find out what they've given him."

Jonah hurried over and took the man by his feet while Michael hefted his shoulders. He could have lifted the man by himself, but the less trauma inflicted, the more time he'd have to deal with whatever he'd been darted with.

Once the guard was settled, Michael took out a tiny instrument from his medical bag, took a blood sample, and started the blood work. It took a moment, but the machine beeped. "A short-term anesthesia. Let's run the makers." His brow furrowed as he looked up the records of drug companies making this formula. Only one. Listed for specific use and limited supply to... "Dr. Jeremy Colvert."

"So, we've got him, again."

Frank's words send a bolt of pure panic racing through Michael. He'd gotten his hands on Clarissa again, and Michael had promised her that would never happen. He knew what Jeremy had done before. She'd shared a lot but more she'd hidden. It had damaged her on such an elemental level that he couldn't see how she'd come out as strongly as she had last time.

"Did you get hold of Daniella?" he asked Frank.

"Yeah. She said her people are working on it, and she'll buzz you as soon as they have a clue."

Hurry up and wait. He didn't do that well. Instead, he started working through the information they had. Colvert hadn't stopped his experimentation once Clarissa had escaped, but found a remote way to oversee his work.

"What's the current capability of a wireless network, Franklin?" Michael asked.

His friend scratched his head. "Depends if they are onsite or nearby. Civilian systems have greater limitations. Depending on the band they're using and the number of access points, they're limited to around three hundred feet. Now, military systems run closer to four hundred feet. But that's of course presupposing that he isn't using a wireless connection over the 'net. In which case..."

Michael scrubbed a hand over his face. If he was using a wireless connection, not just Wi-Fi, then the situation was indeed much more grave than they thought.

"Who do you know..." Michael turned toward Franklin and noticed the brawny man had his communicator open and was tapping away. "Franklin?"

"Just seeing if I can get a friend down to the lab ASAP to take a look around. He'll be able to tell me if he's using Wi-Fi or patching in."

Michael waited for the grunt of satisfaction he knew his friend would give. Within minutes the sound filled the air, and the tension in Michael's body seeped away.

"He'll be there in a few minutes. He's on leave. His wife's pregnant and they had an appointment with the gynecologist a couple of streets over. He'll drop her off to do some shopping."

Michael didn't want to hear that as a mixture of helplessness and terror churned wildly. He just wanted Clarissa back. Whole and unharmed.

COMING to was a terrifying experience and reminiscent of a past Clarissa had sworn never to revisit.

Humiliating, because once more, she was naked and fastened to a cold, hard slab.

"Let me go." Her voice wobbled as she tested her bonds, strained against them. Tears slid down her face, like scorching lava on her chilled skin.

"My dear! You left before I could give you any extra freedoms. You were special. So very special and dear to me." Jeremy loomed over her. He reached out and slid a finger down her cheek, smearing the wet tracks.

It took every ounce of willpower not to flinch away at his touch. It took more courage than she'd ever thought she possessed to remind herself that she'd done her time as a victim. She knew there were people out there looking for her. People who would make him pay for his sins, and that bolstered her spirits somewhat. Clarissa bit her lip and glared at the man watching her.

"That was very naughty of you, Clarissa. You should never run from me, because there is no one who means more to me than you. We always remember our first, don't you agree?" His face lit up with an inner madness that chilled her.

"Let me go, Jeremy. Because when the others arrive—"

"No one will find us, my dear. I made sure of that." He grinned. "Your muscle tone has increased, but so has your body fat ratio. I'll need to do something about that." He started examining her, dismissing her as a human again. Just like he'd done in the past.

Seething fury replaced the terror, and once more she tugged on her bonds, twisting and turning, working on the metal cuffs that held her in place.

"Don't fight it, my dear. After all, I have plans for you. For us. This time I intend to ensure that you have a successful gestation."

The words stopped her struggles. "What do you mean?" Strange, Clarissa thought, how tight and strangled her voice seemed this time and the way she felt as if her body were floating now.

"You didn't think we'd implant viable embryos in order to check if your body would accommodate a pregnancy, did you?" His laugh stole her breath. "That would be a waste. No, we simply implanted some that would have been discarded as unsuitable for implantation."

White lights dotted her vision. *Unsuitable for implantation.* Nausea rose and threatened to choke her. "You bastard."

Again, she began pulling and tugging, calling on every fiber of her being, her muscles rippling and adrenalin surging. Clarissa bared her teeth, and he frowned, paled.

Crack! The sound echoed, and he stepped back. One pace then another. His face strained, and the color leached away.

"I will kill you, Jeremy. If I get my hands on you..."

The atavistic quality in her tone made him pant with fear, and the tang of sheer fright filled her nostrils. Her second hand slammed free as the boom of shattering metal filled the air.

He glanced around, the urbane air he usually wore fleeing in the face of such fury.

Clarissa wrenched at the restraints on her ankles, pried them loose, uncaring of the tearing of flesh and the rivulets of blood that flowed from her fingers, and as she rose, he ran, pelting out the door.

Chapter 15

The building rose like a white cardboard box shrouded by dark trees whipped into fervor by the wind. The howling played havoc with the earpieces as Michael waited, huddled by the door where Franklin stood guard along with three other well-armed men. He felt unnecessary, but if Clarissa had sustained damage, he wanted— no, he *needed*—to be there.

One of the men flung the door open, and the shouts and demands drowned the measured chaos that surrounded him. The surge of those who would clear the building rushed like a heavy tide, and he waited for Franklin to give the okay. He'd been in enough situations to know that he'd only get in the way.

"The front section's been cleared. We can enter."

Michael shoved away from the wall, stalking after the Kevlar-encased man. The suit Michael wore chafed, but he ignored it. It was a minor irritant given his current state of mind.

The hall they entered seemed endless, the doors opened left and right. Each of these rooms represented a stage in the process Jeremy Colvert had undertaken in defiance of the 'No Harm' oath. The people he'd injured in his sick, scientific march into a hideous future.

"Was there anyone in..." Michael indicated to the rooms, and Franklin shook his head.

"No. I figure if there is anyone hidden here, they'll be on a different level. Down below, likely. We've been unable to locate complete records or plans for this building—the records we found initially aren't complete. They're more like future planning outlines. What is clear is that he's clever. He's been preparing for this for a long time, Mike."

Their eyes met, and Michael read what Franklin didn't say. A lot of people had come through these doors in various states, and few —if any—escaped alive.

His mouth dried. How long could this have been going on? How many people had died beneath the butcher's hand? Jeremy had clearly sunk a lot of his financial resources into the building of this private facility, and no one had noticed.

He'd skated beyond the law for many years. He'd have to be made to pay for that.

They padded down the hall, the men ahead checking every room and removing the electronic systems contained within as Michael watched, his insides roiled like a mass of worms as he waited for them to find Clarissa.

Time ticked by. Slowly.

When Franklin's communicator squawked, Michael twitched. "Sir, we can't find the woman you're looking for. However, we did find plans for yet another facility. We just don't know where it is."

His heart thudded somewhere down around his knees. Another facility. Somewhere else.

Michael fought off his dizziness. "They must have found her locator and took it off her. Did they find it?"

Franklin gazed at him steadily. "I don't think..."

"No. It's tagged to her specifically."

Franklin clearly didn't understand; he continued to look at Michael blankly.

"Down the track, anyone thinking to find her..."

"Oh! Oh, right." Franklin depressed the button. "Find the locator. Bring it to me." Michael scrubbed his hand over his face. Two steps forward and three steps back. "Sir! We've found something. You need to see it."

Michael followed the young man who'd been part of the team to a small laboratory.

"What?"

"We found Dr. Colvert's medical records. As in his private ones, sir." The young man hefted several old-fashioned folders. "But this one in particular may be of interest. He's got several bio-cybernetic prosthesis himself. But even more interesting, he's been doing work on alloys and drugs that would neutralize the systems."

Michael swiftly perused the files shoved at him. His smile was grim. "Bring that with you. When we find him, we know just how to hold him." Then he stalked out of the room, his fury still lashing around him.

▭

HE'D SLIPPED AWAY.

"Rotten bastard." Clarissa stilled just beyond the doors and scanned the hall. *Smaller corridor and a different design on the walls and floors.* "Wonder where I am this time?"

She padded forward, the chill caressing the skin of bare arms and legs. The open-backed hospital gown fluttered in the breeze.

At the first door to her left, she stopped and peered within, but all she saw were large canisters. White cylinders with black tops. She wracked her brain, trying to remember where she'd seen this kind of set-up before. Row upon row stood in silent sentinel, and a large gas cylinder sat against the wall, tubing snaking here and there.

She pushed on the door, and an alarm beeped softly, the palm pad glowing. Biting her lip, she backed away, moving silently down the hall to the next door. A similar set-up caught her gaze, and peering through the window, it was clear it was some kind of laboratory. The wall of white interspersed with microscopes.

Yet, for all the set-up, the place was empty. Clarissa considered why this place would be quiet and uninhabited. A little further down the way was a waiting room decked with pictures of happy babies and parents. Realization dawned then. This clinic, where he held her, was for the insemination of women. *IVF.*

Her gut churned now, and she headed for the large, wood-paneled door—sure it led out of the building and to freedom—before stopping. If she went out there like this, she'd be inviting more questions. And it was more than likely guarded. They'd find her, and she'd be back to square one.

"How am I getting out of here?" She glanced around the tomb-like building. It seemed odd that it was so darned quiet. Where had Jeremy gone, and why was there no one else here?

Creeping up the hallways, every muscle tense and ready to flee while her heart thudded, was an exercise in fear. Every door she peered within showed her empty treatment rooms.

Here and there she'd check the ceiling for some kind of surveillance system, but none were evident. A sound echoed, and her breath caught. *I can't afford to be caught.*

She moved faster, looking for clothing and some way to escape. To her left was a break room with metal cabinets. She rushed in, flinging the doors open as quietly as she could, finding a set of green hospital scrubs and a discarded cardigan. In another cabinet she found a set of rubber shoes.

Clarissa tore the gown from her body, sliding on the clothing. Then she turned and continued up the hall until a voice echoed.

"She's in here. Got loose. We have to find her."

Jeremy.

If the voice echoing was coming from the direction she thought, she'd need to move back to the main reception area. Perhaps she could swing up into the ceiling? There were polystyrene type tiles and she could hide.

Fear lent her speed as she hurled herself onto the reception desk and shoved one of the tiles away. Her hands grasped the metal runners, and she heaved herself up before sliding the tile back into position as the sounds grew closer.

It took every ounce of willpower to suppress the heavy exhala-tions that would give her away. *I'm not in the clear yet, but if I stay here long enough, they'll leave, then I can escape.* Gingerly, Clarissa lowered herself down to lie still and wait them out.

▭

IT WASN'T SO MUCH the waiting, as the not knowing.

"We'll find her, man! I know it's hard."

Franklin patted him on the shoulder, and it took every ounce of Michael's attention to still the jerk. They didn't understand. That was the problem. No one else could. She'd been used and abused, subject to the most heinous of testing regimes.

"She's out there and they've done things to her. Things I can't even..." It didn't matter what he said, so he rested his elbows on his knees and leaned into the cup of his hands.

Michael inhaled deeply, welcoming the air expanding his lungs as the tension leached away. Surely there had to be some way to find her?

His mind shifted and swirled, considering the information that he'd gleaned. The lab had results, details of the many varied experiments.

"Jonah? Get my brother on the line." He shoved up from the chair as an idea started to formulate.

"What's up?" Franklin followed him as he stalked to the command center outside the lab.

In his peripheral vision he noted men in tactical suits, who looked up, the color draining from their faces as he ran through the scenarios in his mind, his cyber-enhanced extremities clenching and releasing.

"Sir, we're doing all we can." The officer, *DeVries* emblazoned on his uniform, spoke quickly.

Fear bloomed around him, rich and ripe. A heady aroma it was true, but not one he had any intention of acting on. No, all his energy and concentration was for the one who'd taken Clarissa.

Jonah grinned at him and proffered the phone. "Here."
"David?"

"Yeah, Michael. What's up?"

"I have an idea…"

———

CLARISSA PEERED AND LISTENED. She watched through the tiniest crack in the ceiling as staff and couples came and went. She wasn't game to move much, unsure of the long-term safety of her perch. She'd already determined that the drug they'd given her had kept her under for hours, maybe more than twelve, but the readout in her vision was blurry, as if failing. From time to time, Clarissa dozed as she waited out the day.

With her bladder screaming and thirst raging, Clarissa knew she couldn't wait too much longer. It was only when the flood of people became a trickle that she realized a full day had passed and her opportunity to escape might be nearing.

As the last couple was shown to the consulting rooms, the receptionist stood and swiped her hands over her pants. "Ticky, I'm going to the restroom before I start the shutdown."

Noting there were no others in the room, and with the echo of a voice beyond answering, Clarissa inched back the tile as the receptionist disappeared around a corner. She lowered herself gently onto the desk, reached up and replaced the tile, then headed for the door. Opening it, she slid outside.

Night was settling like a shroud, and she shivered. Winter was almost at its deepest, and she needed shelter. Or assistance. Her feet were only shod in the rubber shoes, which offered very little protection from the freezing conditions. She thought longingly of the thick, leather boots she'd worn until meeting Michael.

At the thought of his name she sighed. If only he were here now.

Her shoulders slumped as she tugged the cardigan around herself and bowed her head. Glancing out beneath her lashes, she hoped to appear just like everyone else in the sea of humanity heading for home.

The crosswalk was crowded, and she carefully pushed to the center, hoping to use the anonymity to get further away. Ahead was the subway and to the left a tiny lane. Which was the best option?

Clarissa bit her lip and peeled off, heading for the lane, looking for somewhere to hide out the night. The subways were filled with the indigent, but they would report her as soon as look at her. They protected their spots with a fervor few understood, and a newcomer had to be prepared to be as forgettable as they were. She stood out far too much.

She plodded as hunger gnawed and the extreme need to find a bathroom became pathological.

"Clarissa!"

She stopped. *He's found me.*

"I will fry you, Clarissa, if you don't come back here. Then I'll do the same to all the others. You don't want that, do you?"

She turned unsteadily, hate and grief suddenly weighing her down, as if he'd attached manacles and chains to her.

"Jeremy, let me go." Her voice cracked, and tears obscured her vision.

"Let you go? You're my first and best. And we always remember them. Come now. Do your duty and I'll spare the rest."

She knew exactly what he meant. He wouldn't kill them. Not on purpose anyway.

"How did you work out where I was?" She ran a hand over her belly even as it gurgled. She took a small step toward him, wondering if she could somehow push past him. Three men, each armed with big, ugly weapons, stood behind him, and she tried to calculate her chances of success in running from them. Pushing past and escaping hovered at the forefront of her consciousness.

Given the cold looks on their faces, her chances were few, but perhaps death was her only way out?

"It was easy once I realized you hadn't removed the implant and left it in the clinic. I didn't know that until you left. Where did you hide, dear?" The echo of the urbane man she'd thought she'd fallen for sickened her.

"In the ceiling."

His gaze bored into her. "Well now, aren't you resourceful? I'll have to consider what section of the brain that is and see if it's possible to build that in the youngsters I'm going to make."

Those words stopped her slow forward motion.

"Let me go, Jeremy. I can't be of any use to you now. I mean, there are others looking for me. Looking for you."

The ugly bark of laughter that echoed in the night had the hairs on her body standing on end.

"You think they'll stop me? I'm not planning on being caught. I have a contract with sections of the government. They want to know how we can increase the chances of building super-soldiers, and you're my template, Clarissa. Now, come along. I'm tired of these games."

Clarissa closed her eyes, inhaled deeply. Opening herself to the wealth of implants, she opened her eyes and settled her gaze on the guards, focusing on the way they held their rifles. Their stances. Similarly, she considered Jeremy. In her mind she sifted through possible scenarios. It took place during the heartbeat as she paused to inhale. Then she tensed her muscles, letting her hands clench before she sprang forward.

A quick and well-placed kick took down the first assailant. The feel of her foot against his genitals, the sudden explosion, and the howl filled her senses as she whirled away. She landed and shoved her fist into the face of the second, while the whine of his gun split the air.

Burn! Her side ached, but she used the impetus to spin into the third man, her elbow connecting with his throat. His gargle ended with the thud of his body on the concrete.

Her momentum halted as she stood in front of Jeremy.

"I'm not some experiment. I'm a human being. I didn't ask for this, but what I will do is end you. You will never enhance or tinker with another human being."

He laughed. "You think it's so easy? It's not. Your little friend, Michael? I know about him and the work of his surgeon. If anything happens to me, the people who own you will go after him. He's no more than a pawn too. A well-placed one, but not above the law. My work will live on in the hundreds of scientists who build weapons for our planet, and you're the one choosing who will be the test subject."

She already knew he had connections. The long tendrils of power had to know what was going on, to enable him to circumvent police and other systems. She wavered, and he reached out. Clarissa didn't see the hypo-syringe until it was too late.

As the darkness descended though, she heard her name bellowed. *Michael...*

MICHAEL SAW CLARISSA slump to the ground before the gnarled man.

"Stay still, Dr. Colvert. You're surrounded." His team swarmed as he headed for Clarissa. "You have no idea what you're messing with, Dr. Villede. My work for the government has given me certain freedoms, and shall we say, I've been rewarded handsomely. You taking her from me won't stop my work. It's too far advanced. Soon, we will see the 21st Testing Protocol bill to the Senate."

Michael screwed up his face as he hunkered down where Clarissa lay.

"What did you inject her with?" Whatever it was, it hadn't affected her breathing, seeing as he could detect a normal sinus rhythm.

"Oh, just a strong dose of a natural sopoforic that won't over-load her sensors. It'll keep her sedated for an hour or two. Now, hand her over, and everything will be right with the world." Jeremy leaned closer. "You'll be richly rewarded for the decision. I'll make sure of it."

When Michael looked up, he noted that Jonah and Franklin waited behind Jeremy Colvert. "Cuff him."

Jeremy laughed. "Normal cuffs can't hold me. I've got bio-cybernetic prosthesis, you stupid boy."

Michael gave a grin that had Jeremy frowning even as Franklin and Jonah set to work. "I know. These aren't normal cuffs. They're enhanced with transmitter dimmers and fashioned from a poly-oxide material. You won't have use of your hands or arms, but it won't stop you from walking."

He scooped up Clarissa, holding her close and thanking the stars that she'd survived and freed herself once again.

Now he wanted her home, safe.

Chapter 16

Clarissa woke, stretching a little and opening her eyes as memory rose. For a second she tensed with fear. Had he caught her again and taken her somewhere new?

She glanced around the room. Knew it as the one Michael had brought her to before. She twisted her head a little and saw him hunched in the chair beside her bed, asleep.

"That doesn't look comfortable." She rose and padded to the bathroom.

Even as she returned, he didn't wake, and she stood there studying him. He was a good man. An honest one. A man she could... Dammit all! She already did love him.

Michael had waited for her permission to kiss her. He hadn't hurt her. He'd tried to protect her. He'd made her feel whole and understood the levels of damaged psyche she carried. She'd trusted him, at least until that meeting in the dining room. The one that had seen her rush from the room and had been her undoing. She'd need to talk to him before she committed any more to a relationship between them. Perhaps she'd read it wrong? Hope told her she needed to ask him.

Kneeling down beside him seemed the most natural thing in the world, as did raising her fingers to his lips. "Michael?"

He muttered and shook his head, and she grinned.

"Wake up, Prince Charming."

His eyes fluttered and then flew wide. "You're awake."

"And you weren't."

"No. I was so worried about you." He reached out and grasped her hand, holding on tight.

"I only found you because of the GPS tracker Colvert implanted."

Clarissa smiled, although she knew it was wobbly at best. "Damn. I didn't think he'd put one in there. I tried to check for one when I first escaped." She shrugged. "I still don't know all the things he did. There were so many procedures. Each, Jeremy informed me, designed to see what the average human could become and survive. I guess I was the lucky one." Memory surfaced. "He has others too."

"We found them. But none of them were you. I worried I'd never find you again. He has... He had clinics all over the place, and I don't know that we'll ever find them all."

She released the pent-up breath. "No. Probably not, but he's got some deal with

government officials, Michael. I think he's also using the IVF clinic to not only fund, but to further his experiments. This isn't a short-term plan he cobbled together."

"Holy hell." Michael turned a shade of green as understanding dawned. "We need to contact the patients. The authorities." Clearly, the ramifications didn't sit well with him.

Clarissa's memory of those short-lived pregnancies had her biting her lip. "Some of them won't agree to termination. If it were me, I wouldn't."

His hand cupped her cheek and swiped at the sudden scalding tears. "I wouldn't ask you to either. It would be your choice."

"I need to ask you about the other day. When you were planning with your friends, Jonah and Franklin. You talked as if... As if using someone for bait would be acceptable. How could you think that?"

"Damn. I didn't mean it like that. What I was thinking was that we could see if Sara would agree to cooperate. We would have secured her enough to ensure that we could trace his transmissions. I wouldn't put her in harm's way."

"Because she means that much to you?"

"She's been a good friend for a long time."

"And more?"

He leaned in, resting his forehead against hers. "Only a friend. No one else since you, Clarissa. No one else will make me need more. You are the woman who understands me and completes me. I don't want anyone else."

"But we've only known each other for a small amount of time. I mean, I knew Jeremy longer and he…"

"He used you. It was always his intent. But mine isn't. I can't promise to be your knight in shining armor or Prince Charming, but I will do everything in my power to protect you. Love you. Give me that chance, Clarissa."

Certainty threaded through her now, and she closed the space between them, seeking his kiss. It was sweet and soft. A caress and no more. Not unless she wanted it. And she did.

Her lips pressed harder, opened, and it was as if the floodgates opened. He wound his arms around her waist, tugging her closer. Inhaling his scent deepened her desire.

She threaded her fingers through his soft hair as he murmured against her lips, "Make sure you know that if you keep this up, I'm going to make love to you."

A grin stole across her features. "Oh, I know, Michael. I do want this."

He surged up, pulling away long enough to shrug out of his shirt, while his eyes kept her gaze prisoner. The sight of his bare chest, the crisscross scars that snaked up and down his arms, only enhanced her hunger for him.

He lifted her, one arm under her legs and the other curved around her back. He carried her to the bed and laid her down, as if she were the most precious cargo in the world. Warmth and love flooded Clarissa. To have waited for the one man, all the long years, made the rewards sweeter.

"I don't…" She gasped as he set to work, unclipping the top they'd dressed her in after being rescued. "I've never done this before, Michael. I'm not so sure…" Embarrassment at her lack of experience wavered in her voice.

He stilled and rocked back on his heels. "You're a virgin?"

His gaze settled on her face, and she worked hard to resist the urge to duck her head. "Uh, yeah."

He smiled, lighting his entire face. "Then this is the greatest gift you could have given me." Even as her top gaped, he raised his lips, traced the line of her face before cupping it and bending in so he could kiss her. "That you are mine in every way that counts, means so much to me. I will treasure this."

Rubbing his lips over hers sent sparks of electricity coursing through her.

She lifted her hands, curling them in his hair before skating down to his shoulders. Wordlessly entreating him to join her, because the molten pool in her stomach demanded that she assuaged the hunger and need that was building.

Clarissa clutched his shoulders as he trailed his mouth down the side of her jaw to her neck. Nerves jumped and her body involuntarily arched, clamoring for release. She whimpered as his hands kneaded her buttocks beneath the loose pants.

"Michael?"

"It's okay." He raised his head, and she noted the ruddy glow of desire on his features. "Whatever you want, it's good. If you don't like something, tell me. This time has to be perfect for you."

A single tear traced down her cheek, and he stopped, frowned. "What's wrong, Clarissa? We don't have to—"

She laid her finger against his lips. "I want to. So much. But you tell me you want it to be perfect for me, and I don't know how to do the same for you." The words ended on a wail, and he grinned.

"There. That made it perfect for me. Because you want it to be right." He crawled onto the bed beside her and gathered her close. "Just let me love you, Clarissa."

With careful fingers, he pushed the shirt from her shoulders, gazing at the flesh he uncovered. Somewhere deep in her body, a coil of desire began to curl tight.

"I'm going to touch you now." He did, sliding one hand from shoulder to breast, where he stilled, cupped her, his thumb toying gently with her nipple. Every move soft and gentle.

Once more she let go of her senses, allowed them to focus on how his caresses affected her, drugged her so that she slid into the maelstrom.

"I want..." She couldn't form any coherent thought as he laid his lips against the supple flesh of her other breast. His tongue flicked lightly, leaving her breathless and hungry. When he opened his mouth and sucked the tip in she was sure she'd explode.

Clarissa gripped his hair, pushing him closer as he toyed with her, releasing his hold and allowing his hand to travel south. He found the band of her bottoms, wiggled his fingers as she moaned, then burrowed beneath the cotton.

Michael raised his head. "You like that."

The guttural tones reminded her that he too had needs. The cool air teased her damp and highly aroused flesh, but she pushed that to the side as she reached for his jacket.

"I'd rather you joined me in this voyage of discovery." She hardly knew the husky voice as her own, but she'd heard that arousal affected every inch of a woman's body. She gazed at his bare chest, and her mouth dried. "I..."

"I take it you like what you see?" His laughter echoed in the room, and she gulped, more than liking her current view.

He reached out, dragged her close, and she squeaked as their flesh mashed together, nerves jumping and quivering.

Between her legs an insistent throb grew, married with the increased heartbeat. Her stomach clenched. "I want you naked, and I want to be naked." Clarissa winced at her bald request, and he laughed again.

"As my lady commands." Michael eased away, and she gave a tiny groan. "I'm coming back."

When she reached to tug down her pants, Michael shook his head.

"No, Clarissa. I'll do that."

The smile he gifted her was wolfish, and her breath caught in her throat as he shimmied out of his trousers, hooked his underwear with his thumbs and removed them too. Totally naked and adorned by moonlight, all Clarissa could do was stare at the man before her.

He slid back onto the bed and hauled her close, his mouth closing over hers. His tongue thrust between her lips as he ravaged her. His firm hands slid over her body, and she drowned in the sensations he evoked.

He dragged her bottoms down until they lay flesh to flesh. When he tugged away from the scorching kiss she heaved for breath. His fingers walked down her torso, across her belly, and it clenched involuntarily.

"I'm going to touch you, Clarissa. Slide my fingers deep inside you." The dark and erotic whisper of his words played havoc with her mind as he did exactly that while every nerve ending quivered at his ministrations.

His fingers brushed against her skin, opened her wide and slid across, so that her legs splayed for his intimate contact. When they breached her, she whimpered and moaned, her hips undulating. "What..."

"Let it go, Clarissa. Enjoy the sensation and know that you're beautiful."

Michael kissed her collarbone, her jaw, then slid down to her stomach, where his mouth caressed her navel. Tongue dipping in and out in the parody of the sexual act. Her fingers curled in the sheets, holding onto the tiny thread of sanity as the world shook around her.

When his tongue grazed her mons she arched and cried out, eyes squeezed shut as shattering sensations crashed down. He urged her on, loving her in the most secret fashion until the quivering of her body ceased and she fluttered, little more than a leaf on the wind.

Her chest heaved. "I don't..." Her wits were scattered, and forming a coherent sentence seemed beyond her.

"You enjoyed that." The rasp of his voice betrayed his desire, and he rose up, like an avenging god, covering her body. "Now it's our turn together."

His lips tasted musky, the scent of sex redolent, and she gasped as he seated himself between her legs.

"Open for me, princess. Let me find my home."

Instinctively, she wound her legs around him, and he moved, flexing his hips so that he slid a short way into her body. The unfamiliar sensations washed over her. It was the same as when his fingers... The thought died as he flexed once more and slid more deeply.

Her breath hitched. "I don't..."

His lips found hers again, and this time his tongue slid within in time with the movement of his body seating himself. The pressure, unfamiliar and yet so erotic, thrust her back into the wild storm of passion, and he moved, hands gripping her hips and helping her to find the rhythm.

Movement. Sound. Scent. It all came together as she crested a peak she'd never known existed.

He twisted his mouth from hers. "Oh God. You feel so good."

The words egged her on, and their wild dance sped up, became wilder until her body splintered.

"Michael?" She couldn't help herself as she fell.

He stilled, clutching her close, and she felt the jerk and dance deep within her body as he came.

Stillness descended. Her arms around him. He clutched her close. They were still joined as they sucked in shuddering gulps of oxygen.

"It's never been like that before." His voice shook. "I love you, Clarissa."

<hr>

Chapter 17

<hr>

Morning came, a muted light rising above the horizon, while Clarissa lay on the bed, considering the night just passed. Beside her, Michael slept, his body relaxed while her own continued to tingle in reaction to their wild lovemaking.

No one had ever told her that she'd feel so deeply after sex. Only, it hadn't been just that. Her heart was fully engaged.

She'd fallen for Michael. But as damaged as he might be given the results of his actions, would it be fair to continue with this situation knowing how many demons she currently carried around in her mind?

She bit her lip and contemplated the sunrise.

"Was it so bad?" Michael spoke softly, and she started.

"What?"

"You're frowning and have the sheet tucked up under your arm as if you're either embarrassed or regretting last night."

She stared at him, aware that he too was unsure of his ground. "I... No. I'm just wondering if there is any way we can be together, given I'm not exactly a prize."

He scooted up in the bed and reached out. Clarissa ducked into his embrace. "Clarissa, you have to know I love you. I wouldn't have stayed with you, or for that matter shared what we did, if my emotions weren't clear. I don't toy with women."

"It's not that, exactly. I just don't know what it will take to find me again. You've got your problems, but mine seem bigger. Now, saying that out loud, I sound shallow, don't I?"

"No. Just unsure. We'll work it out together. However, as much as I want nothing more than to show you—just like last night—how much I want to be with you, we should shower and dress. Jonah and Franklin need to get home. David and Daniella are due to join us for breakfast, and there's supposed to be a debriefing of the team who found you."

She screwed up her face. "A debriefing?"

Michael laughed. "Yeah. We need to find out what more was discovered, what Jeremy was able to share and the results of all the various reports the government guys found in the clinics. Including the IVF one they held you in. And yes, he fessed up about that."

"So the GPS tracker, that's how you found me?" She needed to know how and why.

Michael groaned. "You're going to want to know it all, but table this discussion until breakfast. Now come on. Get up. It's time for our shower."

She pinked a little at his careless suggestion of 'our', meaning he'd be sharing with her. "I, uh... My robe is..."

He swung her up into his arms. "You don't need it." Then he swiftly marched to the doorway to the ensuite before standing her on her feet. "I'll start the water."

She watched as he opened the door to the shower and engaged the water, his buttocks firm along with the acres of skin she'd touched. On a whim, she grazed her fingers over his back, and he hissed. She pulled away in time to see him turn, the desire from the night before clear on his features again.

"Do that again, and breakfast will take a lot longer."

Understanding now that he was as affected by the hunger between them gave her a sense of power, and she grinned. "I might have to remember that."

"Do. Because that won't be the last time."

MICHAEL WATCHED CLARISSA OVER BREAKFAST, his gaze settling on her still slightly swollen lips. They hadn't made it through their shower without an interlude, and while she claimed her body wasn't a little sore, he'd noted the faint change in her gait. He'd have to be gentle next time. Ease her into the intimacy.

"How is Clarrie?" she asked.

Michael could tell she felt guilty taking this long to ask about the old man, and he reached out, clasping her hand in his. Luxuriating in the warmth of her touch.

"He's fine. Been demanding regular updates on you. You'll get an opportunity to talk to him later today. I'll arrange a vid-link if you like. He's going to the main ward tomorrow, but Sara will keep an eye on him for us."

"I'm so pleased." Clearly though, she labored under a heavy load of concern.

"That's not all that's bothering you, is it?"

"No. I'd like to help him out. You know, he's got nowhere to live." Sadness clouded her gaze.

"He has somewhere to stay. He'll be staying here, unless that's not what you want?" "Oh, could he? I mean, if he wants to." The hope in her eyes warmed the center of his soul.

"Yeah. I'd do anything for you, Clarissa."

Her smile was like a ray of sunshine and for a moment he basked in it.

"I was going to see if I could find a unit for him, somewhere nearby. Of course, if he

decides he wants to live by himself, we can do that too. But I'd like him to reconnect with his family. He only left them because he thought he was a burden. But now he knows he's eligible for assistance..."

Her grin widened. She took a sip of her latte, the froth settling on her lips, and he licked it away.

His body tightened again, and he couldn't control his grin at the memory of her taste and the way she responded. Her gaze widened, and for an instant, a flare of the flames that were never quite doused around her flickered hot, warming him through.

"You're looking particularly pleased with yourself, brother dear." Daniella slid into the seat on his right.

He scowled but brushed away her comment. "None of your business, Daniella."

She sighed. "You do know a lot of things have changed since we found her, don't you? The government is adamant that you both must be controlled." He opened his mouth, and she lifted a hand. "I've tried to tell people that you're not involved and she's merely a pawn. They won't listen to me."

"Make them hear what you have to say then. We have done nothing wrong."

Daniella sighed. "I know that. You know I am aware of the issues, but I'm a single senator. Even with me calling in every favor owed I'm between a rock and a hard place. However, President Yin owes me a couple of favors, and I called them in. The military had connections with Colvert. There was an agreement. I can't totally circumvent it, but I can unravel the string a little."

Daniella cleared her throat, and everyone at the table, including his brother, Jonah and Franklin, Clarissa, and the three agents at the end, stopped and waited.

"I have a directive from President Yin," Daniella announced. "The situation is this. Colvert had an agreement with the military—or at least the more extreme factions—to investigate and enhance cybernetic implantation to create super-soldiers. The agreement is legal and must stand."

Clarissa whimpered and David growled, but she stopped their reactions.

"Yin has given me the opportunity though to, shall we say, find and rehabilitate those who've been affected by Colvert's treatments."

Michael's gaze narrowed on his sister's face. "What does that mean?"

She scowled. "Agent Fairburn? Your findings from the clinic please."

He blushed and shook his head. "They're bad. We've found out that these experiments have been taking place for years. In fact, there are notations going back over ten years of implantations with an organic-based cybernetic growth hormone."

Michael stared at the man, unsure if he understood correctly, because the implications were huge. "An organic-based cybernetic growth hormone? You mean he can grow children with cybernetic systems?" Revulsion slammed into Michael.

"Yeah. And what's more. The first viable specimens were implanted nearly eleven years ago. The first crop of cyber-enhanced children were born ten years ago."

Nausea and disorientation flared.

"Thank you, Agent Fairburn. This is not the only case of his experimentation. He was using the clinic to grow warriors as much as to fund his other experimentation. However, after reviewing Clarissa's file, it is our belief that he was also hoping that those with cyber enhancements would be able to carry and deliver at full term another generation. In short, he was creating an entire new species. One that the military would ultimately employ. Or at least those pre-disposed factions." Daniella shook her head and Michael sat watching, struck dumb by the far-reaching ramifications of her announcement.

Super-soldiers, home grown. With cybernetic implants. It made sense now the breadth of the implants Clarissa carried. He glanced at her, his gut churning at the whiteness of her face. He reached out to her, and she inhaled deeply.

"So, Daniella. What's needed of me?"

Michael silently cheered, well aware of how much those words cost Clarissa.

Daniella blushed a deep crimson. "Actually, it's both of you. And those of us here at the table." She waved her hands at those assembled. "Yin wants a high-level team created to find these children and those who have engaged in this experimentation. He wants to rehabilitate the kids before it's too late and those radical groups get their hands on them. He wants the experiments shutdown and the results contained. I've been tasked with heading this up at a political level.

This is to be strictly off the books. Michael and Clarissa, you will spearhead it. You're the only ones who understand the emotional and physical results. You're also the only ones who could probably deal with the kids. Jonah and Franklin, you are being co-opted to the team. Officially you will be drafted to Yin's personal protection squad but loaned to my staff. Agents Fairburn, McNally, and Sevres will be the investigators. David, I need you on hand as the senior officer. Resourcing will be discretionary."

"What if we choose not to help?" Michael's lips felt stiff as he watched Clarissa struggle with her emotions.

"Don't, Michael. I have been instructed that should you choose not to cooperate then your status will be reviewed. Not my words, brother, but the threat and implication are something I don't want to consider."

He shoved away from the table. "I need time. So does Clarissa."

Daniella watched him, her face grim. "I can give you twenty-four hours, but I need your answer tomorrow. Think hard, because you two aren't the only ones affected."

In that moment, he was sure he hated Daniella. Michael stalked around the table and reached out to Clarissa. "Let's get out of here." He steered her out the front door to the garage, where a sports car sat. "Time for a ride." He ushered her in then got in and ignited the engine. As they roared out the gates of his house, he turned to her. "Where do you want to go?"

"I don't care. So long as we're together."

The engine revved as they drove onto the road and far from the crowd.

⬚

"WE NEED TO DISCUSS IT, MICHAEL." Clarissa cradled the warm drink in her hand as they gazed out at the city below. "I know."

"We can do a lot of good. I mean, I can't easily get into teaching if there is danger, and until all these people are caught, there'll be no rest for either of us."

Looking at Michael was easy, she guessed. But the danger scared her. That she could lose him, and the hope and love she'd found could be stripped away, along with the chance of a shared future, left a hollow feeling in her stomach. It left her and them both with so few options.

"What if we wanted to, you know, have..." Her mouth dried, aware she might have read too much into his declarations.

"Kids? I do, with you. But they could be in danger if what Daniella said was correct. But it doesn't feel right that because of an accident or something beyond our choice should be the reason we accept the role they demand us take on."

She shook her head. "No, it's not right. But neither is the situation the kids find themselves in. And Daniella is correct. There is no one else that understands what they're up against except us."

Michael ran his hands through his hair. She really did love him. It wasn't some kind of momentary blip or because of last night, wonderful though it had been. They'd made a commitment. To each other. That had scared her but hadn't stopped her. Neither should this.

He sighed. "You're right."

"We should go home then. Let them know what we've decided." Clarissa started reaching for the seatbelt, but he placed his hand on hers.

"Wait. Before we do, I want to ask you something." The tremor in his voice stilled her fingers and she swung back, their gazes colliding.

"What?"

This time his exhalation betrayed his nerves, and she frowned. "If we do this, I want us to be together. I won't let them send you off in one direction and me in another. I don't want to lose you. Clarissa, would you marry me? Stay with me through whatever the fates throw in our way?"

A chink of light warmed her soul. "There's no question for me. I will."

He leaned over the console and kissed her softly. "Good. Then let's go lay down some ground rules. Put on your seatbelt, princess. We're going home."

She laughed as he revved the engine.
Home. The sweetest word of all.

If you enjoyed this book by Imogene Nix why not check out some more of her titles by scrolling through to the following pages?

In the darkness evil waits...

As a young bride Kira was whisked away from everything and everyone she knew, including her new husband and became Christina, an operative of the Displaced Persons Unit.

As the danger grows she sees an opportunity to save her

husband Vasya and sister Serina. But nothing is the same. Serina is grown up—married and pregnant.

Vasya too is older and darkly forbidding. Trusting Christina doesn't come easily until a catastrophic event takes place. Now, knowing the truth everything he thought he knew is changed. But at a very high cost.

The four must work together to defeat the Demon, Zuor and the stakes are higher than they imagined and all could be lost.

The burning at the back of her neck warned she was being watched. A quick glance didn't clarify it. Instead, she turned around in time to see her mother's face, pale. "Mama?"

She took a step forward, but her grandfather snatched her wrist.

The grip was painful, and Kira stilled. "Let your parents talk."

She didn't know what the topic of conversation was, but it couldn't be good.

The dappled sunlight seemed cooler than before.

Her father crooked his forefinger at her grandfather while they stood there. For a moment she wished Vasya had come with them, but he had to work. Just the thought of her new husband warmed Kira.

She only had a few minutes to contemplate her newly defined status as a married woman, when her grandfather pulled at her hand. "Come with me." He tugged and, confused, Kira allowed herself to be towed away.

A glance at her parents' faces stole any feeling of well-being.

"Grandfather?"

"Shh, my love. You must go." His grip was implacable and his face stern, but he shivered.

"What are you doing? Where are you taking me, Grandfather?"

They moved rapidly through the village they'd visited to sell their wares just that morning, and for the first time since they'd arrived in the market place she felt fear. What was wrong? Was it something to do with Vasya?

"You are in danger. We must send you away." The words confused her further. Send her away? Danger?

"Where is Vasya?" She stumbled over a stone, but he kept tugging her onwards.

With a quick glance around, he hauled her into a dirty laneway between the buildings. Kira gasped, trying to drag air into her starving lungs. "There's no time. We must get you away."

A nondescript shopfront lay ahead, and he pushed on the door. It rattled and opened with a loud groan. "Andre? Andre, are you here?"

An older man shuffled into the room, bent nearly double from the weight of the load on his back. "Marat? What do you want?"

"My granddaughter. They are coming for her and us. Get her away. Take her now, while you can."

The man's face clouded over. "Are you sure?"

"Grandfather, where is Vasya?" Fright had the blood in her veins pounding.

"Hush, my precious. Andre will see you well." He turned. "Whatever it takes, Andre. Take her now." With surprising speed, her grandfather whirled and was gone.

The man, Andre, eyed her. "Come this way, child. There is no time to be lost."

Eleven years later

The tattoo of her heart and cry of terror woke her, as they usually did. Once again, as she had since that rapid flight from those who sought her, she found herself in a lonely bed. Hundreds of miles away from everything she'd dreamed of, in a house she'd built for them to share. As always, it left her wishing that Vasya had fled with her.

Instead, here she was, exiled without her husband. With a sob, she rolled over and let the tears fall.

Available from Beachwalk Press
books2read.com/IOTB

Direct Autographed Copy
http://bit.ly/2w6g4K6

When Cupid—otherwise known as Diocail— is banished from his home on a remote Scottish Island, he's set a series of tasks by the great god Lugh, who also happens to be his father.

In **Blame The Wine**, he must bring two lovers together... BBW Cara and James, the man she's lusted over from afar who happens to be a super geek and head Veha Industries.

In **A Stranger's Embrace**, Diocail is driven to help an

emotionally fragile Jane and Davis, a famous author. The task is more complicated, with the existence of Carstairs her could-be ex-husband and teenage daughter, Frannie.

In **_Revenge on Cupid_**, Diocail must take the ultimate chance and find his own happily ever after with Simone. Sometimes the past gets in the way and HEA's don't come cheap though.

The dusty, dingy little diner was full, even with its current state of cleanliness—or lack thereof. People from the surrounding offices didn't care about anything except the incredible, well-prepared food at a reasonable cost. They flooded in, like waves to the shore. As one tide left, another swept in.

"Honestly, Simone. I'm going to try getting his attention one more time. If that doesn't work, I'm out of there. I mean, how long can I keep trying?" Cara picked at the caramel tart she hadn't been able to resist with the cheap metal fork and flicked the blob of fresh cream that sat on top to the side of the plate.

"You've said that tons of times before. Besides, what are you going to do to get his attention? Hmm? Walk naked through the typing pool?" Simone bobbed the straw in her smoothie as she eyed her friend with a frown. "It's been what? Eighteen months since you saw him, and you've mooned over him from a distance ever since you met him. You need to move on, Cara. That is, unless there's something you haven't shared?"

The query was arch. Cara shivered even as she shook her head. "No."

Simone quirked an eyebrow, obviously unconvinced with the answer. Cara let out a deep sigh of frustration. "There's a position...it's only temporary, for a PA reporting directly to him." She speared a forkful of tart, chewed quickly and swallowed, before continuing. "In his office, full-time for the period of the engagement. I saw the memo yesterday. I mean, I have the skills, right? I can type, answer phones, make coffee, file, greet people. What's more, I can probably do it better than all those size eights in the typing pool that Ms. Jackman seems to prefer." She nodded thoughtfully. "All I have to do is get past the ogre in Human Resources."

Simone stared at her, disbelief clear on her face. "Girl, I so remember that woman. If you think you can get past her, you're doing better than I ever did. That's why I left Veha Industries, remember? Maybe it's time to haul out your resumé and consider some other options. Look for something better." Simone shook her head and billows of her crimson hair swirled through the still air.

Cara understood Simone only had her best interests at heart. But this time she knew the outcome would be different. Hell, she could feel it in the air. The tingle of expectation.

"Cara, the HR ogre will hang you out for breakfast before she offers you anything like a position in that office. Remember her mantra? Good looks and good work make for a positive workplace!"

Simone didn't sugar-coat anything. It was another great reason for their long- term friendship. Honesty. But Cara didn't want to hear the truth in the statement. Even if it was exactly as her friend said.

Cara nodded quickly. "Yeah, I know, but if I don't try, then I won't know how close I can get to him, right? And the only way to catch his attention is to get past *her* and see him in person." Cara quaked a little at the information she needed to share. The favor she needed to ask. "Anyway, I tidied up my resumé and dropped the application into a memo envelope yesterday, so it's too late to back out now. I mean, fortune favors the brave. Doesn't it? If I don't snag an interview, I'm going to visit the career advisor across the street and register with them." She shrugged. "I'll look for temp work until something more long-term shows up. I can see what they have on offer and well...who knows? Maybe a job with the right boss is just waiting for me. But I'd rather this worked out, to be honest." Her voice trailed off into a whisper. "I really wish he would notice me."

Simone took a long slurp of her banana drink, and Cara noticed her questioning gaze even as she squirmed. Finally, Simone nodded. "It's your funeral. So anyway, you'd better show me this memo if you want me to be a referee for you. I'm guessing that's what you need, right? I'll have to know what I'm supposed to say about you before they ring."

Cara smiled. "Thanks, Simone. I knew I could count on you." She slipped a piece of paper out of her handbag and handed it over. "Sorry it's a bit creased. It was in the bottom of my bag, I stashed it so none of the others from the pool would see. You know how it is."

Available from Love Books Publishing
books2read.com/CelticCupid

Direct Autographed Copy
http://bit.ly/2vs7wtS

Can a cyber-enhanced warrior and a ship's captain find love together?

Levia Endrado never wanted to be a warrior, but at seventeen she was deemed suitable for battle. After intense training and multiple enhancements, which gave her superior strength and healing ability, she was sent off to defeat the enemy—a killing machine with a mission.

When the war was over, she had to find a new life. At twenty-seven she's a washed-up veteran without a future. Or she was, until she met Sandon Daria.

Serving as a pilot aboard Sandon's spaceship the *Golden Echo* makes Levia long for a different and gentler life. But old hurts and even older enemies aren't so easily forgotten. Particularly when they come back for her.

Sandon is determined to show Levia that she's more than just a BioCybe…she's the woman who completes him. Getting close is just the first step, keeping her alive is an even bigger challenge, but one he's willing to take because the prize is their combined future.

Levia scanned the long line of other hopefuls entering the chamber. The large building in the center of town was cold, and she dragged her wrap around her body, even as she craned her head, looking to the high ceiling. She'd never before had an occasion to enter the testing complex, yet she'd seen the lines of teenagers every time they passed the building.

Once she'd asked her parents why the teens were lined up and her mother's face had shuttered. Her stepfather had just shaken his head and growled. They'd stopped her questions with a carefully uttered, "You'll know soon enough, Levia." The pain in her mother's eyes had been enough to shush her questions. For endless months afterward, her parents had traveled different routes to the educational facility she attended and Levia lost interest in the puzzle of that building.

Now, as she looked around, remembering that long ago spring day, it was her opportunity to find out. But she felt a surge of concern at what lay ahead. She likely wasn't the only one, given that there were probably two to three hundred seventeen-year-olds gathered in the one place. Ahead of her, she caught sight of a couple of girls, their arms linked together and wide smiles on their faces.

Scanning the crowd, she became aware that, by far, a majority of those gathered displayed both fear and trepidation.

"All female subjects will enter through doors three, six, and seven. All male subjects will enter through gates four, eight, and ten." The speaker above her was loud, and she jumped before checking the numbers etched on the black metal sign over her head.

The massive doors beside her swung open, and now an uncertain silence reigned. Many of the youngsters hung back, clearly discomforted by whatever testing regime lay ahead. This was where they'd been told their futures would be determined.

"Oh gosh, I hope they only have an aptitude and psych eval. I don't think..." Levia turned to see the white face of the girl behind her. The girl had uttered what many must silently be thinking.

Levia dragged an unsteady breath in, her hand resting flat against the plane of her belly as she looked around. No one had entered yet. It was clear many were on the verge of taking the step, but still they hung back.

She straightened her shoulders. "I'm not afraid." It was always wiser to approach things head-on, she believed. When her biological father had died, she'd been one of the few to view his capsule before it was sent into the massive gray structure built to accommodate those who'd moved onto the next life realm.

Her legs shook as she wobbled toward the entrance. Beyond the doorway, she spied sealed cubicles and her heart stuttered. Why cubicles? Usually testing—med and psych—were in eval-units, hidden only by billowing white curtains. She glanced back, noting that others had taken the first step.

"Move along, subjects." Once again, the androgynous voice of the address system blared.

Of course, given it was her seventeenth anniversary of birth, she was technically considered an adult now.

She thought longingly of baby Rald and her half-sister, Elda, waiting at home for her to return, and the celebrations to be held that night. That made her smile. She would need to make them proud of her.

She entered a row and the tall Educational Specialist, the edu-specs as her peers laughingly called them, stopped her. "Present your credentials to the scanner."

She'd done this many times since the tiny implant had been slipped below the dermal layer of her skin at birth. The small unit in her wrist heated as her details were checked.

"Enter the first cubicle, Levia Endrado, and follow the instructions to complete your assessment."

Thus dismissed, Levia moved to the first unit, laid her palm against the scanner, and the door slid open soundlessly.

"Welcome, Levia Endrado. Take your place in the eval-unit." The soft contralto of the voice echoed after the door closed silently behind her.

"What are you evaluating?" Her voice was breathy, and she peered around.

"Your skills—physical and psychological. Your emotional and medical status. Your educational attainment levels."

It was an answer that shed little insight into the many things she was hungry to know. "Why do all seventeen year olds—"

"Take a seat, Levia. Then we may begin your testing."

If she'd expected an answer, she was sadly mistaken, she considered sourly. She dropped into the seat, the soft leather-like surface molding to her body.

"Levia Endrado, you are required to remove all non-specified apparel."

She jolted in the chair. "It's cold."

"The temperature will be amended. Remove the non-specified apparel."

Her misgivings grew as she dragged off the light wrap she'd brought with her, and then threw it to the floor at the side of the unit.

"We will begin, Levia Endrado. At any time, should you experience any malfunctions of the unit, simply depress the red button." It glowed and she grimaced.

Levia reclined against the chair and waited for the testing to begin.

The first examination was based on her understanding of the

political system, where she saw herself, and her knowledge of the rights and responsibilities accorded through citizenship of both her planet and the commonwealth.

The second test was mathematical and scientific proficiency. It felt like hours had passed by the time she'd finished, and she lay limp on the seat, exhausted.

"Levia Endrado, you may rise. The sanitary unit will emerge once you trigger the yellow button at the door. Should you require refreshment, press the blue button and a restorative will be made available."

"Can I leave?"

"Negative, Levia Endrado. Your needs will be catered for in this capsule."

"Why?" Her voice hitched and true fear rose for the first time. Why did they keep her in the alcove?

"All will be revealed at the end of the testing cycle."

Levia looked at the now empty screen before hurling a curse word. It was met with silence.

The urgent throb of her bladder reminded her that she needed to use the facilities, so, with

a sigh, she rose and clambered from the seat. After attending to the needs of her body, she walked around the unit, peering at the door, but it was obviously programmed remotely. She poked and prodded, but it made no difference. With a huff, she headed back to the chair.

The moment she'd settled in, the viewing screen shone bright. "Welcome back, Levia. The next sequence will evaluate your psychological reflexes, then that will be followed up with the general knowledge portion of the evaluation."

"When can I leave?" It seemed better to ask bluntly, she told herself.

"Once the examination is completed. After the next set of evaluations, you will be subjected to the physical aspect."

"Then I can go home?"

"Levia Endrado, you will now complete the psychological test. This will be undertaken by one of the center's personal evaluators."

She frowned. Personal evaluators? She bit her lip, and the sting reminded her that this wasn't something to joke about. In her seventeen years, she'd only heard of personal evaluators being brought in once before, and that was when one of the girls at her academy had been in a serious accident. Both legs were amputated and her body's ability to keep her alive had been gravely compromised. Her peers had been informed that the girl had requested the assessment before she could request her support systems be disconnected.

"Levia Endrado, are you ready to recommence processing?" The emotionless voice echoed once more and she gulped.

"Yes."

Available from Beachwalk Press
http://www.beachwalkpress.com

Direct Autographed Books
http://bit.ly/BioCybe

Also by Imogene Nix

<u>**Warriors of the Elector**</u>

- Star of Ishtar
- Starline
- Starfire
- Star of the Fleet
- Starburst
- The Star of Eternity

The Star of Ishtar & Starline - Print

Starfire & Star of the Fleet - Print

Starburst & The Star of Eternity - Print

<u>**Blood Secrets (Re-releasing 2020)**</u>

- The Blood Bride
- The Illuminated Witch
- The Sorcerer's Touch

<u>**The Search Duology**</u>

- Miss Elspeth's Desire
- Miss Isabelle's Craving (Not Yet Released)

<u>**Reunion Trilogy**</u>

- War's End
- The Assassin
- Executing Justice

The Reunion Trilogy in Paperback

<u>**Sex Love & Aliens**</u>

- Tangled Webs
- False Webs
- Covert Webs

21st Testing Protocol

- Cyborg: Redux
- Children Of A Greater Evil (Not Yet Released)
- When Evil Came To Stay (Not Yet Released)
- Finis: The War To End All Wars (Not Yet Released)

Celtic Cupid Trilogy

- Blame The Wine
- A Stranger's Embrace
- Revenge On Cupid

The Celtic Cupid Trilogy in Paperback (August 2019)

Zombieology

- The Reset (2018)
- I Dream of Zombies (Coming 2019)

Single Titles

The Chocolate Affair

A Sapphire for Karina

BioCybe

Hesparia's Tears

Tomorrow's Promise

A Bar In Paris

Inheritance Of The Blood

The Plan

Loving Memories

Hero of Heartbreak Hill

Raspberry Dreams (Not Yet Released)

Non Fiction

Self Publishing: Absolute Beginners Guide (With Suzi Love)

Written as Ciara Cave

25 Curated Ways To Get Rid Of Telemarketers

Book Signings for Absolute Beginners

About the Author

Imogene is published in a range of romance genres including Paranormal, Science Fiction and Contemporary. She is mainly published in the UK and USA.

In 2010, Imogene Nix (the pen name not Imogene herself) was born. Imogene sat down and worked tirelessly for 3 months culminating in the book Starline, which became the first in a trilogy titled, "Warriors of the Elector." Since then she's had over 30 titles published and is now focusing on hybridising herself - with a mixture of traditionally published and self-published works.

In fact, she's taking control of many of her back catalogue books, which are slowly re-releasing as self-published titles.

Imogene is a member of a range of professional organisations world wide, and believes in the mantra of mentoring and paying it forward and is actively involved in mentorship (through NaNoWrimo and her vlog: In The Chair With Imogene Nix) and tutoring of new and upcoming authors.

In her spare time she loves to drink coffee, wine & eat chocolate and is parenting her spoiled dog and a ferocious cat along with her husband and 2 human daughters and looks forward to weekends away with her husband in their caravan "The Seven Year Hitch!" Do look forward to her caravan romance at some point!

To Contact Imogene

www.imogenenix.net
imogene@imogenenix.net

facebook.com/ImogeneNix

twitter.com/ImogeneNix

instagram.com/ImogeneNix